WATER CRAZY

WATER CRAZY

by

EDNA WALKER CHANDLER

DUELL, SLOAN AND PEARCE
New York

First edition

Affiliate of
MEREDITH PRESS
Des Moines & New York

Library of Congress Catalogue Card Number: 62-8529

MANUFACTURED IN THE UNITED STATES OF AMERICA FOR MEREDITH PRESS

VAN REES PRESS • NEW YORK

CONTENTS

U. S.1179300

WATER CRAZY

1.

THE RUNAWAY

Fins Harper was running . . . faster than he had ever run in his life. And Frank Harper, better known as Fins, had no intention of going back to that crowded classroom.

Talk of the coming tests, which he knew he wouldn't be ready to meet, had taken most of the class period.

Suddenly he knew he couldn't take another word of that talk. Something seemed to snap inside his head, and he had to get out.

The next second he was out of the class, dogtrotting down the hall. He could hear his best friend, Mel Dawson, calling him. Mel had kept him in class before, but this time he wouldn't go back, not even for Mel.

Now he was still running, and there was no real need for it. No one was after him.

But just ahead was the river . . . that good old, cool, friendly river. And in his hiding place under the willows were his fins, his snorkel, and that shiny new mask waiting for him. With luck he'd have an hour to dive before time to go on his paper route. That was enough, anyway.

Just thinking about what he had in that hiding place under the willows had put speed into his feet. Fins Harper was no longer running away from something; he was running toward an hour of real living.

The river was a restless thing, and its very unrest made it cloudy sometimes. But it was a good place to practice and get ready for the really big places.

Fins tossed his clothes on a branch, pulled on a pair of diving shorts, slipped on his fins, put on the mask and snorkel, and he was off.

Boy, what water! What soothing coolness! There was just nothing like it anywhere.

This little cove was quiet and deep, the rocks big and sheltering, and today the water was clearer than usual. Of course, it was never as clear as some of the better diving places like Carmel and Laguna Beach, and the really far-off places he'd read about. But for a river, it was good, and it was near enough that he could get to it often. Fins and this river were friends. They had known each other for a long time.

Fins cruised along on the surface, his snorkel feeding him the air he needed. He took a short, quick dive now and then, coming to the surface to blow out the snorkel and look around.

On his third trip down, a big bass came near, swam

lazily around him. Fins could have touched the big fish, but he didn't. In his mind, he talked to it instead.

"Boy, you're a beauty! Too smart for the fisherman's bait for a long time or you wouldn't be this big. Well, you keep on being smart. I wonder how big you *could* get."

"Well, I'm going up for air, Mr. Fish. You don't need it, but I do."

Fins came to the surface, blew out his snorkel, and looked around. Someone was near his clothes! Someone who was also putting on diving shorts—Mel. That's good, he thought. Now I'll have someone to swim with me.

He knew he shouldn't dive alone. Everything he'd ever heard or read told him that. But he'd done it lots of times and nothing ever happened. If a fellow remembered the safety rules, he'd be O.K. Of course, the first rule was, NEVER DIVE SOLO. Oh, well . . . he'd break that rule this time and keep all the rest. That ought to do it. Now, thanks to good old Mel, he wouldn't be breaking that first rule.

But then, if you want to dive so badly that it's about all you think about, how can you always have a buddy along? No one he knew liked underwater sports as much as he did. Sure, Mel could dive. Good, too, and he had fins and a snorkel and mask, but Mel could take it or leave it alone.

"Come on in, Mel! Water's fine. Sure beats that final exam talk!"

Mel stepped out from the rocks, bent for a surface dive, and disappeared. In a few seconds he was coming up beside Fins.

He shook the water from his face and said, "Boy, are you a goon! Taking off like that so near the end of school! You already have a whole bunch of cuts against you. You'll be doing night school to make it up!"

"I'm not going to any night school! I'm done with the whole business of school. If I don't care about my credits . . . and I don't . . . no one will make me do time in night school!"

"You mean you'd quit school this near the end of your second year in high? You're almost through high school, and now, just because you got fed up today, you'd throw it all over? How crazy can you get?"

The anger in Mel's blue eyes made no impression on Fins. He'd been through this before, and always he'd listened to his friend.

But Fins was being extra stubborn this time. Every hair on his short-cropped head seemed to stand up for fighting. He stuck his chin up, and the anger sparks flashed in his dark eyes.

"Look, Mel," he said, his voice carefully controlled against the rising temper he felt, "I've gone back to school before because you wanted me to, and Mom wanted me to, and Mr. Corliss—he's a good egg—talked to me too. I've gone back and kept hoping that I could see some use in it. But it's just no go. The math and science are pretty good, but that history and English . . . I just don't dig that stuff. It's a big fat waste of time for me."

"But you have to have history and English this year,

and then next year you get more choice. Someday you might have to write business letters or give speeches . . ."

"Who, me? Give speeches? Write letters? Not on your life! No use talking about it, Mel. School just doesn't have a thing for me, not for what I want to do."

"You really know what you want to do?" Mel asked.

"Sure, I know. And I'm almost old enough to do it now too. I want to go out with skin-diving crews, and bring up stuff that nobody else can get. I want to see what's down under. I want to go down farther and stay down longer than anyone has ever done before! That's what I want to do!"

"You don't even have a lung!"

"I know, but I'm saving for one. My paper route is getting bigger, with all these new people moving in, and I'll have a lung before summer is over, I'll bet!"

Just then the boys heard a rustling on the bank. They glanced back at the spot where they had put their clothes. Someone else was there.

"Now, who has found our special place? You didn't tell anybody, did you?" Fins demanded.

"Of course not! We'd better get back. Some jerk may have ideas about taking our clothes!"

They swam toward shore as fast as they could.

The person on the bank made no move to leave. He just sat, waiting.

"It's Mr. Corliss!" Fins exclaimed.

Of all the people he might have seen right then, Mr. Corliss was the last one Fins wanted to see. For Mr. Corliss, the boys' counselor, was a real good egg. It was hard to answer his arguments and stand up against him. Some of the teachers he could talk right back to, and it was fun, even when he knew he'd get in trouble for it. But not Mr. Corliss. He seemed to get a fellow right where he lived, and there was no defense against him.

But he won't talk me into going back to school this time, Fins vowed to himself. This is one time I've really had it!

"Swimming pretty good, Frank?" Mr. Corliss called, as the boys paddled up to the bank.

"Sure, it's always good," Fins answered, his voice a bit on the stubborn side. "A lot better than a stuffy schoolroom."

Mr. Corliss looked thoughtfully at the dark-eyed boy floating lazily at the edge of the water.

Fins's body was cooky brown from long hours in the sun and water. He was tall and looked older than his fifteen years. Too bad his face was so often filled with anger and rebellion. It would be a good-looking face, actually a handsome one, if he could only let a few more grins take over. His dark, short-cropped hair usually looked uncombed, giving him a belligerent look. Too often his brown eyes flashed in anger or smoldered with stubbornness.

Mr. Corliss's silence made Fins uneasy. He swam with nervous, short strokes, waiting for the counselor to begin his usual lecture. But Mr. Corliss didn't say a word. He just sat there, looking serious.

Suddenly Fins couldn't bear that silence any longer. He swam up to the river's edge and pulled himself up on a rock.

"Mr. Corliss," he said, "I guess you're trying to think how to get me back to school. I can tell you right now it's a waste of time—yours and mine both. Mel, here, has been working at it, but this time I'm done, finished! I can get what I want without more school . . . without another single day of it!"

"Yes, I know that's what you think," Mr. Corliss answered, "and I could argue with you, but it wouldn't do any good. You see, teachers can get tired too. Just plain tired of arguing with stubborn kids! And I think I've reached that point!"

Mr. Corliss's voice had taken on a hardness that Fins had never heard before. Could this be the kindly boys' counselor of Del Rio High talking like that?

"Yes," Mr. Corliss went on, "I think you've reached the place where the school might as well give up. Only we can't. If you quit school, the truant officer will be after you because you have to finish high school or stay there until you're eighteen, which you aren't by three years. You see, the law takes it out of our hands at a certain point."

"Then I'll run away!" Fins said defiantly.

"Think what that would do to your mother," Mr. Corliss reminded him. "It's hard enough for her to see you do all this swimming and diving when she lost your father as a frogman in the war. If you ran away, she would have nothing left. Some kids would do it anyway, but I don't think you will."

The picture that Mr. Corliss put in his mind was complete, and suddenly he knew Mr. Corliss was right. He couldn't run away. So what next?

He wasn't to wonder long.

"Here's what we can do," Mr. Corliss went on. "You come back to school and I'll help you make up today and all the other cuts against you. You're smart enough, and you can make the grades if you even half try. That will keep the truant officer out of your hair—"

"But I'm not coming back to school!" Fins interrupted. "No matter what, I'm not!"

"Now, wait—let me finish. This will end your high-school life, since you want it that way. Your mother is a widow, and I'm sure she could use your help with the food and clothing bills around your house. We can help you get a job, and you can stay out of school on a work program, based on your mother's need. After you're eighteen, the school has no more responsibility toward you. But it does mean you will have to come back to school for the rest of the year—six weeks more—make up your cuts, and take your exams with your class. Then the school will back you on this work program and that's that. How about it?"

Fins shrugged. "Well, I guess I don't have much choice. I don't want to spend the next three years dodging the truant officer and the juvies. I'm not THAT bad! I just don't want to waste the next two years in high school. I want to get on with diving. Someday I want to do some real important job in skin diving, and I'll do it without high school!"

"Anyway, you're going to get a chance to do it your way," Mr. Corliss said, with a grin. "So long, boys. Be seeing you next Monday."

Mr. Corliss started back to town.

"Well, he did it again," Fins mumbled, "sweet talked me into going back to school."

"Just to finish the year," Mel reminded. "I don't see how you can do anything else now and keep out of real trouble, and you don't want that kind of stuff."

"No, I guess not," Fins agreed, "because I couldn't do much diving if I got picked up and stuck in one of those juvie places. He had me over a barrel, all right. I didn't know it would be like that. But anyway, this work plan sounds good. I can work, help Mom with expenses, and still get in a lot of diving."

For the first time in a long time, Fins felt happy as he thought about the days ahead. Only six more weeks of school and then he would be done with it forever!

Then it was him for the sea, the best diving spots in the world; his friends would be other skin divers, and he'd live with the fish, the coral, and the kelp!

What a life!

Fins carefully boxed his diving things and hid them again. He knew Mel wouldn't tell anyone about their secret place, and he was practically sure Mr. Corliss wouldn't.

He and Mel put on their clothes and headed for home.

Six weeks, and no more school for him! Fins Harper was through with school forever, or would be soon. The words beat a merry tune in his head as his feet raced on.

2.

THE SCUBA CLUB

THE next six weeks went faster than Fins thought they would, and now it was mid-June and school was out. His friends scattered to all parts of the state and beyond, for vacations, camps, jobs, one thing and another.

Mel got a job as part-time helper at the Spring City swimming pool, so he would be in town as always.

Mr. Corliss had talked to Fins's mother about putting Fins on a work program when school began again.

At first, Margaret Harper was set against it.

"What's so bad about getting a high-school education, Fins?" she asked. "You just have to have that much to get any place these days."

So Fins had gone all over it again, with his reasons for leaving school, and sometimes it was hard to keep his temper down when his mother brought up all the usual arguments for school. She didn't have hair that was "pushing red" for nothing!

And he was just as determined in his own way as his mother, even without the red hair.

"Why don't you get a job like Mel has?" she asked.

"You're waterlogged most of the time, anyway. That kind of a job ought to suit you fine."

"Because," Fins explained, "there is only one job like that in this town and Mel has it. Besides, my paper route makes more money than that, and it's building up fast. And I'll have more time to look around and get lined up for a job this fall if I'm not tied down to a summer job."

"And," his mother said, "it will give you more time to live with the ducks and the fish, and those odd characters in that skin-diving club you want to join. Oh, Frank! Why don't you take your swimming a little less seriously? Everybody ought to learn to swim—I wish I could—but to dive and go down where men were never meant to be . . . that's something else. Fish and octopus creatures and slimy old seaweed and . . . and sharp coral belong down there. Not kids like you."

His mother's eyes were shiny with tears that always seemed close to the surface when she got to talking about diving. Just thinking about it made her get upset like this, and she could find words and arguments that packed a bigger wallop than you would ever expect from the one hundred and ten pounds of her.

"Look, Mom," Fins said, "I know why you feel this way. It's 'cause Dad was a frogman in the war and he didn't come back from one of his undersea missions. That's been rough on both of us, but worse on you. It's meant that I don't know what it would be like to have a real family, as Mel has, and most of the fellows I know.

"I was so little I can't really remember Dad. Sometimes when I look at all those pictures you have, I think I do remember, but then I know I don't . . . not really.

"But I think I know how he felt. I like to think of all the wonderful things he saw down under. I like to remember that he was doing a big job for his country, for all of us, and he was doing it in the way he liked best. Some of the fellows had to do things in the war that they didn't like at all. But Dad was a frogman by choice. I'll always remember that. Just as I choose to be a skin diver.

"Sure, I could stop with being just a plain good swimmer. A lot of people are like that and they like it that way, but the world under the water—it thrills me, Mom. It pulls me like a . . . well, sort of like a magnet, I guess. I just have to go down and find out. There's something about things down under that makes you feel all peaceful and part of real big things. And look, Mom," he went on, "be reasonable! How many times have you ever heard of skin divers drowning?"

Margaret Harper was silent. Right off she couldn't think of any, except one big swimmer who had gone off with the frogmen and hadn't come back.

"Just your dad," she said. "Losing him was enough for me, and it ought to be enough for you."

"Well, Mom, that isn't enough to scare me. Tonight is the first meeting of the summer for the SCUBA Club in town, and I'm going to join, if they'll have me. I hear they have some stiff rules in that club, and they might not take me in, but I'm going to try. See you later!"

Fins grabbed his jacket and was gone before his mother could raise any more objections.

At the Y, Fins looked around at the people who, like himself, had been interested enough in skin diving to come out tonight. They were nearly all ages, though no one was younger than he. There was one boy who looked about his age and a young couple a little older. A boy and his girl friend out for skin diving, probably. The rest were in their late teens and up, with several as old as he was, or older.

A husky young man, about the age of Mr. Corliss, called the meeting to order.

"I'm Newt Browning," he said. "I'm the swimming and diving instructor here at the Y. Some of you know me. Now I want each of you to give your name and tell us why you're here."

Some wanted to go spear fishing, others wanted to study sea life in its natural surroundings, but most of them just liked skin diving as a sport.

Bob, the boy with his girl friend, wanted to learn to do underwater photography.

His girl, Betsy, had a different reason.

"I want to be a skin diver so I can keep track of Bob," she said.

A friendly chuckle went around the room.

"You see," she went on, "he gets down there and he forgets his meals; he forgets he has a date with me, and he'd forget his head if that lung didn't hold it on so well.

He gets sort of carried away, if you know what I mean. I'm going to learn skin diving so I can keep him from getting a real case of raptures!"

The chuckle became a laugh, and Fins joined in, but one thing puzzled him. What did she mean by "raptures"?

"It could happen," Newt Browning said. "It almost happened to me once. But if you know the signs you can feel it coming on and get yourself to the surface before it's too late."

"Just keep Bob above the hundred-foot level, Betsy. Put a rope on him and drag him up if he goes lower!" someone suggested, laughing.

"But he wants to go lower! That's the problem," Betsy answered. "But if he knows I'm along and I'm going where he goes, he won't go so deep because he doesn't want me down so far. That way I'll keep him where he won't get raptures!"

"Dame's tricks!" one boy called out. "They don't cheat fair!"

"Seriously, though," Newt Browning explained, "raptures of the deep, or nitrogen narcosis, is a real danger at great depths. The best way to keep from getting it is not to stay long at depths over a hundred feet."

"But you miss a lot of good stuff that way," Bob said.

"Then your best bet is to get into the gear for real deep-sea diving, with your hoses and all that. But then, you lose the freedom a lung diver has. If you go too far down in a scuba rig, which, as you all probably know, means self-contained underwater breathing apparatus, you'll be

likely to do just what Betsy says . . . get yourself so slap-
happy you will go off playing with the fish and not wanting to come back. That's why it's called the raptures. Great
depth brings a feeling of relaxation, happiness, and well-
being—something like a drunk gets in the first stages of his
drinking. But if he drives a car up a telephone pole or
tries to cross the tracks in front of a moving train, he's just
as dead as if he hadn't been so happy. So you'd better stay
in a depth where this won't be likely to happen."

So that was what raptures of the deep meant!

Fins had no more time to think about raptures, for now
it was his turn to speak. He swallowed hard and looked
around. Speaking before people wasn't easy, even when
it was just a little thing like giving his name and telling
why he wanted to join this club.

At last he had his long legs unwound and braced under
him. Then he heard himself talking.

"I'm Frank Harper," he said, "only my friends call me
Fins, mostly because I've always liked the water. I want
to be a skin diver because someday I want to earn my living doing important diving jobs."

He sat down, and the warm feeling around his neck
began to go away.

Everyone had a turn telling why he or she wanted to
be a skin diver. Then Newt Browning talked about the
rules of the club.

"No diver in this club goes off diving by himself," he
said. "That is the first and most important rule." If anything happened to one of our divers and he was alone, no

one would ever know just what or how it happened. Soon our club would have a bad name among other skin divers if we let our members do those things.

"No member of this club goes down under until he has made a perfect score on check-out of himself and his equipment. For most of you, that will mean taking the training course that starts next week. If you are a good swimmer already and have done quite a lot of free diving, it won't take long to check out. But you must have a perfect score on check-out. Any score less than a hundred is the same as failure in here! You don't just barely pass a skin-diving test. You pass perfect or you don't dive—not with us, anyway.

"We take a lot of trips together to the best diving spots in the country, and we have a lot of fun. First, we work with our scuba outfits here at the pool. When most of the class has checked out at the pool, we go out on a trip. But only experienced divers go down the first time. Then each experienced diver takes a beginner with him. By the end of this summer, if you've gone on all the trips and really worked at diving, most of you should be diving anywhere that it's wise for a lung diver to go. Any questions?"

There were dozens of questions, but Fins didn't ask any. He just listened hard and got his head so full just by listening that he thought it might pop any time.

After the questions, Mr. Browning called for order again and he said, "We have a little job ahead for tomorrow. I would like to have Bob Grant, Hank James, and Rich

Morton work with me on it, but anyone can watch who wants to."

"What's the job, Newt? Any dough in it?" Rich asked.

Rich was a big, square-shouldered fellow with a roving eye. He was the one Fins had first noticed as being a little older than himself.

"No, Rich," Newt answered, "no dough. Just the satisfaction of doing something for the law. There was a holdup and robbery last night along that street where the houseboats are docked.

"One of the owners of a grocery store in the west end of town had taken his money out of the till, intending to bank it this morning. The robber got excited, shot at the storekeeper, but hit a stack of soft-drink cases. The bullet hasn't been found, nor the gun. The robber took the money, which was packed in a small metal lock box, and ran.

"The cops picked up a fellow that answered the description given by the man who was robbed, but he had no gun, no money box on him. The cops think he saw the squad car coming and tossed both the gun and the money box into the water along Harbor Street, thinking he would get some one to dive down later—for a price. I told the chief of police that I could find men to help before the robber's friends have a chance to get on the job. How about it?"

All three who had been named were eager to go, and all over the room hands waved wildly for permission.

"Come along, if you want to watch," Newt said. "We'll

be at the dock about eight in the morning. There isn't anything secret about it, but please don't invite all your friends. Too many people around will make it go slower. So just club members may come."

That means me, thought Fins, as he took out the dollar he had brought for his membership fee. When he paid his dues, Newt Browning talked to him about his plans.

"Glad to have you, Fins," he said. "Something tells me you are going to get along fast. That brown skin shows you've done a lot of water work. That's what it takes— hours and hours of practice, and a real love of the water."

"Yes, sir," said Fins, "I'm kind of water crazy, I guess. I just never get tired of it."

"Good! You'll get a lot of it this summer. When school begins you won't have so much time for diving, but the weather isn't as good for it then, either."

"School won't bother me, Mr. Browning," Fins answered. "You see, I'm not going back to school."

"You mean you've graduated from high school? You don't look old enough for that!"

"No, I haven't graduated. I just plain quit!"

Fins could feel the old rebellion coming into his voice. Would this be someone else who would try to sweet talk him into going back to school? He had just better not!

"How are you getting away with that?" asked Newt. "You're not eighteen, I'm willing to bet!"

Fins told him about the work program and his mother's need.

"But your mother would want you to go on to school,

wouldn't she? I'll bet she doesn't go for this plan! You'd better think what you're doing to yourself—and your family."

"Listen, Mr. Browning! I'm counting ten to keep from getting mad! I have thought it all over and I didn't come here to get a lecture about school. I want to be a top-notch skin diver, and that's all. Someday I want to earn my living on a diving crew. Now, do I get that membership card, or don't I?"

The friendly talk around Fins stopped as his voice became sharp with anger. In a matter of seconds, everyone in the club was listening, but Newt Browning could not be rattled.

He had seen Fins's kind before. Most of them got through this stage of fighting everything and everybody. Once in awhile one didn't get through it without bad scars.

Would Fins get scars? Who could tell? Only Fins himself could ever find the answer to that one. Right now Fins Harper wasn't looking for answers. He had them!

Newt Browning signed the membership card, gave it to Fins, and said, "So long, Fins. See you at the dock in the morning then."

A few called out as Fins made his way to the door, but somehow Fins felt he had got himself off on the wrong foot with this bunch.

Why do I always have to shoot my mouth off at people? he thought. More than anything else he wanted to be in good with Newt Browning and this club. Right now he felt he had messed up his first and best chance.

How dumb can you be? he kept asking himself, as he pedaled his way home through the dark streets. The street lights laughed at him, and the stars, when he could see them, jeered from above.

He could still see them up there laughing at him, those silly jeering stars, when he felt himself going off to sleep.

3.

STAND-BY DIVER

Fᴵɴs was among the first to get to the boat harbor the next morning. For it was here that Newt Browning had said they would meet Captain Barber of the city police force.

Three club members stood talking by the dock steps. One was Rich Morton, the big fellow with the restless eyes.

"Hi!" called one of the others. "Come on over! I saw you at the meeting last night. Glad to have you in the SCUBA Club. My name is Hank James, and here is Bob Grant—he's the guy with the girl friend who is learning skin diving so she can keep track of him!"

Everyone laughed, but Bob didn't seem to mind.

"Betsy didn't come this morning," he said. "She isn't scared of a place like this harbor. Nobody could go far enough down here to get even a touch of raptures."

"She's right," Hank agreed. "You're more likely to tangle with a bunch of tin cans and old oil drums down there."

Hank went on making Fins feel welcome. No one said a word about the way Fins had blown up at the club.

24

"This is Rich Morton," Hank said. "Rich picks up a lot of loose change with his diving. Bob and I have other jobs, and we just dive for fun or to help out when we can, like the job this morning."

"Well, I'm going down this morning too!" Rich said, a flash of anger coming to his eyes. "I don't always ask for dough to dive!"

"I didn't say you did," Hank said. "I just mean you seem to have a knack for knowing where to find the pay jobs. That's O.K. You're just smarter than we are, I guess. Well, Fins, these fellows are all good divers, among the best in the club, and you'll see them at work soon."

"Pleased to meet you," Fins said, "all of you. I'm Fins Harper. Maybe you remember from last night. It's sure good to be here! And I want you guys to know I don't blow my top all the time! It's just that I get so tired of lectures about school and I thought another one was on the way!"

"Don't you worry a bit about Newt lecturing you, or anybody else!" Hank answered. "He'll give it to you once, straight, the way he feels, or he tells you a rule once, and that's it. He's a great guy, Newt Browning, and he makes up his mind about things, but he never rides the guys who don't see things his way. If it's a club rule he has to put across, he does it, but he doesn't lecture about it."

Before Fins could answer, Bob said, "You must like diving. You're brown as a South Sea sponge diver, and this is just the beginning of the diving season here."

"I never really quit diving, even in the winter," Fins

answered. "Ice doesn't close the streams or lakes here, you know, and there are lots of good places to dive in the winter. Anybody that can't stand that much cold is kind of a sissy!"

Fins felt the air grow a bit chilly, and once again he wished he'd kept his mouth shut. Why didn't he ever know when he had said all he needed to say?

Hank said, "Well, I don't think any of us in the SCUBA Club are what you would call sissies, but we just don't get much fun out of diving when we have to fight cold water. It's true that ice doesn't close our diving spots around here, but water that's below sixty degrees can get mighty uncomfortable. Someday we'll all have neoprene suits, and then our diving season will be longer. Any SCUBA would dive in the winter without a neoprene suit, if there's a reason for it, but we don't do cold-water diving for fun. You can have it!"

"I didn't mean it like it sounded," Fins said. "I'm sorry I said that."

The others grinned in a friendly way, and everything was O.K. again. Just then Captain Barber drove up to the dock. Two other officers were with him. Just back of him came Newt Browning in a bright red sports car. Before they were out of their cars, two more loads of SCUBA members drove up and stopped.

"Good morning, Captain Barber," Newt said, "I guess everyone is here who planned to come. Three of our best divers are going down this morning. They'll be ready in a few minutes."

"Good morning," Captain Barber greeted all of them. "I want you to meet a couple of my deputies, Pete Grandon and Charley Jacobs. Pete is the man who caught the thief, and Charley is a good gun man. He knows a lot about the habits of fellows who carry guns and what a gun might do when it is tossed away. Pete and Charley will figure out the best they can about where the gun might be."

"Of course, you know," Newt reminded him, "that anything as small as a pistol or revolver will be hard to find in a place like this. It will be harder than it would be out in the open lake or near the seashore. The men will find a lot of junk down there, and a gun could slide into the slime and get under an old can or something, and we'd go by it a hundred times and never see it. Visibility is very bad in places like this. But we'll do our best."

"Good!" Captain Barber said, full of enthusiasm for the job ahead. "That's all we want, just a real good try. We know the chances are bum, but I've been surprised a lot of times at what you fellows have been able to do under water. Maybe this will be another such time. That gun is all we need to put this thief in jail for another ten years.

"The insurance company will be very happy if the money shows up, too, but that would be too much good luck.

"Locking this thief up again is the most important thing," Captain Barber continued. "He's a man with very sticky fingers. You see, he's out on parole, and he's already broken parole by robbing this store. If we can prove he had a gun, too, we have a real case against him. He claims it was just a man-to-man fight and he had no gun and no plan to use a gun. The man he robbed says he did have a gun, but we have no proof. No gun, no bullet, no money in his possession. You have to have proof, even for a thief on parole from jail."

The divers who were to go down had been getting ready in their cars. Now they were all set except for putting on their diving gear.

Newt began checking them out.

Fins watched every move.

"O.K., Hank. Your air is a little low, but you have plenty for what you are doing this morning."

"Right."

"Bob, you're O.K. I'm glad you have a weight belt that's easy to get rid of. I'll always remember the poor fellow who thought he had such a good thing when he put on weighted shoes for diving. Worked fine several times, better than the belt. Then once he got down farther than he realized. His air began to get low, and he had to come up fast. But he couldn't. Those heavy shoes held him back."

"What happened?" Fins asked.

"Another diver, two, in fact, went down after him, but it was too late. No more heavy shoes in my diving crew."

Suddenly Newt saw Rich's new lung.

"Boy, that's a good lung you have! The best, I'd say! You've been lucky with pay jobs lately, I guess."

Rich's eyes twinkled, but he said nothing.

Newt went on with his instructions.

"Now, you fellows are all set to go. The gun isn't very likely to be down deep, unless it's away out in the harbor. That doesn't seem likely in this case. Come up when your air is about half gone, and if the gun hasn't been found by then, we'll talk about what to do next.

"Captain Barber and I will go out in the boat and keep track of your bubbles. We have two extra tanks of air, so everything is O.K. Now, Captain, where do you think we should start?"

"My men think that the area between those two houseboats is a good bet. The robbery was about there . . ." he pointed to a red X on the dock. "About twenty feet this side of it sets the *Mary Ann*. About twenty to thirty feet beyond is the *Starlight*. The thief was caught about even with the *Starlight*. But he had no gun on him. He got rid of it somewhere between those two houseboats. We have gone over every inch of the dock between those spots, so it has to be in the water, but where in the water is something else. This is where you fellows start guessing along with us."

"O.K., fellows, we're off!" Newt called.

Hank and Bob and Rich went down the ladder and slid into the water. In a matter of seconds, Fins saw their bubbles coming to the surface. He tried to decide which trail of bubbles belonged to which diver, but that was impossible.

Newt and the captain got into the boat and pulled away

from the dock wall, but not far away. They, too, were watching the trails of the bubbles.

It was the longest half hour Fins had lived through for a long time. Now he wanted to be down there with those men, hunting through the junk for a very important gun!

I'll just bet I could find it, too, he thought. I've found things smaller than that under water. Pennies and things. It could be under a layer of sand and slime, but I think the bottom here is pretty hard. I'll bet that little old gun is just lying there, waiting for somebody to look under the right pieces of bucket or something. If Newt would only let me go!

In the next minute or so Fins was doing some really wild thinking.

How can he stop me? I have my fins and mask here. I always take them when I go near the water. I could put 'em on and get in before he'd even know I was there. I could go down ten or fifteen feet and stay a minute, anyway, and that could be long enough, if I went to the right place. Gee, I wonder if I could!

Fins felt a glow of daring rising inside of him. Somehow he had the feeling that Newt wouldn't go along with his plan, so he wouldn't tell Newt. After he had found the gun, everyone would be so glad they would forget a little old thing like a broken rule.

The deputies were watching the boat and paid no attention to Fins.

Fins went to one of the cars, climbed in, and began

getting ready for a dive. He stepped out on the dock just as Newt pulled in with the boat.

Gee whiz! I didn't know they would come back this soon! he thought.

Newt looked at Fins with a cold, fixed stare.

"Going somewhere?" he asked.

Then Fins told him, with words that came so fast they almost tumbled over each other to be said.

"I could go down ten or fifteen feet," he said, "and the way this harbor is, that might be enough. I can stay down with my own air for a little over a minute, and you can do a lot in a minute or so. I have brought up lots of stuff from the river bed in less time than that. Let me take a try at it, Mr. Browning!"

Newt was quiet for so many seconds that Fins thought he was turning to stone. Then he said: "Are you ready to turn in your membership card, Fins? If so, then I have no more responsibility for what you do!"

"You mean if I do a little old thing like going down on my own I can't be a SCUBA member? That's lousy!"

"You heard the rules last night when you joined," Newt reminded him. "No diver goes down on any kind of SCUBA mission without first proving that he can dive, and he must make a hundred per cent score on the check-out list. You haven't had a chance yet to prove what you can do. All we have is your word for it. We believe you can, but you're going to have to live by the rules, same as all the others do. Now think about it. If making this dive is more important than getting in on future SCUBA activities, then go ahead."

Fins said nothing. He stood for a moment, looking out over the muddy water of the boat harbor. Rules! Rules! Every place a fellow turned he ran into a mess of rules!

At last he turned to Newt and said, "O.K., Mr. Browning, you win, but I don't like it!"

"That's your privilege," Newt Browning answered.

Just then Bob's head showed above the water at the ladder. The men were coming out. No one had found the gun, so they went into a planning huddle with the officers.

Fins edged closer to the group so he could hear. That much he could do, at least.

As he listened, he knew they were missing the best bet. He had been down under along every inch of this harbor wall and he knew almost every old piece of junk down there. Finally, he couldn't keep still any longer.

"Look, Mr. Browning, a gun like that isn't very big but it is heavy for its size. Right?"

Newt looked at Captain Barber, who answered, "Yes, that's true." He added, "And the fellow was probably running when he threw it, so he couldn't aim his throw very well."

"O.K.," said Fins, "and he'd want to throw it where he might get some diving friend of his to go down and get it for him later. It wouldn't be easy for a guy like him to get hold of another gun so he'd do his best to hang on to this one."

"Sounds like good thinking," the captain agreed.

"Now, if I'd been that guy, I would pick a spot ahead of time where I would toss the gun and the money if I had to get rid of it in a hurry. Now, look at the dock along this part between the *Mary Ann* and the *Starlight*. What do you see that's kind of an easy thing to see, and not too far away from the dock?"

All eyes followed Fins's pointing finger along the water line at the edge of the dock.

"All I see that's different is that broken oar tied up to that scraggly willow," said Bill.

"Sure. That's what I wanted you to see. Somebody expected to fix that oar maybe—or could be the thief himself tied it there."

"I doubt that," said the captain. "This thief doesn't have the kind of brains that would think ahead that far! He might spot a thing like that when he was 'casing' this place and watching the store he meant to rob, but I don't think he'd go so far as to tie that oar there to mark a spot. That would be hard work, and this fellow is against hard work!"

They all laughed. Then Newt spoke.

"You know, I think Fins has some good ideas there. And he does know this harbor. Why not go down over there and think where you'd be if you were a gun or a box of money that got tossed over right at the spot above the broken oar!"

The divers laughed, checked their tanks again, tightened the straps, and started down. Newt and the captain got into the boat and followed them.

Fins lay on his stomach on the edge of the dock just above the broken oar. He watched the three trails of bubbles intently. I know it's a mess down there, he thought. But if they'll just turn some of that junk over I'll bet they'll find it. Once that gun hit bottom or got caught in something it wouldn't go any place.

The minutes went by. Five—ten—fifteen— Every minute dragged with a weight of shot on it.

At last something happened! The bubble trails got all mixed up together, and the water began to move as the three divers started for the surface.

Newt pulled the boat in with a few quick strokes of his oars. "Looks as if they might have something!" he said.

Sure enough! First up the ladder was Hank, and in his hands was the gun, a dirty, slimy gun, but a gun. He handed it to Captain Barber.

"There you are, sir!"

The captain took the gun, looked at it, and gave it to one of the deputies.

"That it, men?" he asked.

"Sure could be," one of them answered. "We'll check it with some loose bullets we found in this guy's flophouse room."

The other two divers were coming up the ladder. First Hank, and then Rich, holding the money box.

The captain could hardly believe his eyes.

"Boys, you are really good!" he said. "I never dreamed you'd find both the gun and money. We'll get right back and phone the story to the paper. I want people to know about this!"

"Well, fellows," Newt said to his divers, "you did a good job. Finding things like a gun and a small metal box in less than an hour and among all that underwater junk is a good day's work. But I think Fins here gets a little credit for thinking out the broken oar angle. Fins, you'll be a great SCUBA, with eyes and head that work like that!"

Fins began to feel good about life again. Once more he was straight with Newt Browning. He would try his best to keep it that way.

"Thanks, Mr. Browning," he said.

"Newt is the name, Fins."

"O.K. . . . Newt," Fins answered, with a grin that took up most of his face.

"Come out to the lake this afternoon about one o'clock and I'll check you out myself," Newt offered. "This isn't check-out time, but a fellow as anxious to get going as you are ought to have a little break!"

"I'll be there!" Fins promised.

And he was, right on the stroke of one o'clock.

Newt showed him how to put on a lung and take it off, and all the other things he would have to know about skin-diving gear.

Fins checked out on everything but handling that lung.

"You're a fine swimmer," Newt said, "and your breath control in free diving is tops. You do need some more work with this lung. Those things are tricky at first, and you don't get hold of it all at once. I'll give you permission to go down on free dives with the club, but we'd better have a few good workouts on this lung before you go on a diving trip with us. I want to take you to a lake up in the hills where we will find different kinds of diving conditions. How about coming to my house tomorrow afternoon and we'll go on up for a real workout?"

"I can come any afternoon you say, Newt," Fins answered. "My paper-route work doesn't begin until about 4:00 P.M."

"Fine! I'll see you tomorrow then, and in no time we'll have you doing everything any skin diver can do with a lung."

Fins ran home on feet that hardly touched the ground. His papers had come, and he got right at the job of getting ready for his route.

A line on the front page caught his eye.

SKIN DIVERS RECOVER MISSING LOOT AND ROBBER'S WEAPON!

It didn't take long for Fins to read that story! A line at the end looked very good to him. It said, "A stand-by diver, Frank Harper, put his knowledge of the harbor to good use when he figured out almost the exact spot where the gun and money box might be."

Fins felt a thrill of pride as he read the story a second time. At last he was part of a real diving crew—a crew that did things!

4.

CHECK-OUT

THE next morning Fins told his mother how close he had come to checking out with a lung.

"But you have no lung," his mother said.

"Newt rented one for me," Fins explained. "He'll rent one for me today too. Won't be long until I can buy my own. I have more than half the price now."

Although he forced his voice to stay calm and peaceful, he could feel the fight building up in him. He knew his mother wasn't going to like the idea of his getting a lung of his own. Not one little bit! But now that he had joined the club, he'd be getting more and more involved with diving activities. He had stopped using his hiding place at the river, and now he kept all his diving gear in his room. No use trying to keep his plans secret anyway, since he had joined the club. He would just be honest with his mother and then try to keep her from worrying.

"I just don't see why you have to go in so deep with this diving stuff," his mother said protestingly. "Why don't you save your money for a little car? You can get a driver's license when you're sixteen, and that isn't far off. By that time you'll have enough to get a cute little jalopy."

"But Mom, I don't want a 'cute little jalopy.' I want to be a top-notch skin diver more than I want a car. Sure, I want a car someday. Any fellow does. But first, I want a real good lung."

Fins felt his mother's worried, intense look boring right into him. He was sorry he couldn't make her see his need to dive. It wouldn't be any use to promise to quit diving, for it would be a promise he couldn't keep. He would just have to be careful and try to keep from doing real crazy things that would give her cause to worry.

"Don't let yourself brew up a storm, Mom," he said. "You want me to have a car. O.K. How often do you read about car accidents? Every day, don't you? And some of them really mess people up. With skin diving, it's every fellow taking his own risks. Your life doesn't depend on what some other dumb bunny may do or not do. I feel a lot safer down under the water than I do in a car on some of these busy highways, believe me!"

Mrs. Harper had no argument against that, for she had often been upset by the dangers on the highway. There wasn't a good reason at all to bring up against Fins and his thinking about skin diving . . . only that lonesome feeling away down inside because of that frogman who had not come back. She just didn't want the same thing to happen to Fins.

But because she could think of no good argument

against what he had said, she watched him leave the house with only a last warning.

"Well, be careful, Fins. I guess that's all I can say . . . all it will do any good to say. Only I won't be surprised if you come back someday with real fins and scales instead of brown skin!"

Fins laughed and said, "I can think of worse things that could happen to me!"

He picked up his bag that held the mask, snorkel, and fins, and left.

" 'Bye, Mom . . . see you!"

The door slammed, and now the only sound Fins heard was the soft crunch of his bike wheels as he pedaled along toward Newt's house.

Newt wasn't there yet, but Fins didn't have long to wait.

He leaned his bike against the porch and put the padlock on the wheel. Then the red sports car turned the corner and stopped in front.

"Hi, Newt!" Fins called.

"Hi, Fins! I'm calling your bluff today, fella! Only I'm almost sure you'll measure up!"

Fins looked puzzled, and just a little unhappy. What did Newt mean? Calling his bluff?

Newt didn't keep him guessing.

"You see, Fins, a lot of fellows, especially the ones about your age, want to get into full diving rig right off. They think they will be hot stuff just because they can swim better than average in the local pools. They may be right. Most often they're not. If they are half as good as they

think they are, the six weeks' diving training goes fast, and
then they really can do some hard dives. But most of it is
bluff and brag. Then I put them in the beginning classes
and make them start from scratch. I have an idea you will
be able to do what you say you can, or close to it, but in
this business we don't guess. We know.

"So I'm taking you today to one of those little kettle
lakes up in the hills. It's about an hour's drive from here.
We'll do all we need to do and have you back in time for
your paper route. If you can do what I'm going to ask you
to do there, then you can go on any diving trip with us
that you want to go on. If you can't . . . well, you'll be a
student for a few weeks, that's all."

Fins's eyes sparkled. He was no longer unhappy, or
angry, or puzzled. He was thrilled to the bottom of his
toes. He didn't know for sure if he could meet all these
tests or not, but he was sure ready to try. If he couldn't,
then, like Newt said, he'd be a student for a little while
and that would be O.K. too.

"O.K., Newt. Sounds great to me! Let's go!"

"Put your things in the car, and we're off!" Newt said.

In a few minutes Newt's car was eating up the miles
toward the lakes . . . up and up, around one ridge of hills,
and around a small mountain and down. Up and down
they went, and around, but always higher and higher.

"I've never been up here," Fins remarked. "What did
you say is the name of this lake we're going to?"

"It isn't the name of a special lake," Newt answered.
"These mountains and hills were made by glaciers thou-

sands of years ago. Sometimes a glacier was stopped by change of climate, or for some other reason made a very little turn in its course. In making the turn, it dug a hole in the earth. When the glacier was at last all melted, these holes must have looked like big kettles set down in the ground. They filled with water, and people who study these things still call them kettle lakes. The water is clear and pretty cool, even in summer. I brought neoprene suits for both of us, because it's still much too cold for regular skin diving."

"Is it hard to dive in a kettle lake?" Fins asked.

"It's no place for a beginner," Newt answered, "but I think you are no beginner. Besides, I'm with you. I know this lake pretty well. I'll start you in the easy places and we'll go on from there."

Fins felt a big bump of curiosity growing in his head. This was the first time he'd ever heard of kettle lakes. A lake was a lake, either muddy or clear. It was either full of fish, or it wasn't. It was good for diving, or it wasn't.

Before he had time to get his curiosity into a question, Newt was speaking again.

"We may see a few pleasure boats on this one," Newt said. "It's one of the bigger kettle lakes, and the water is clear and quiet so people with boats like to come here. Sometimes fishermen come, but I don't know if fishing is good or not. I've seen some lake fish in it, but I don't know how it is now.

"This lake is probably a hundred feet deep at its deepest point. Now, you aren't going down that far. Not today.

But we can find so many different kinds of diving conditions here that this is a good lake for testing a diver. The
depths vary, with the shore sloping, but not too fast in
most places. There are big rocks along some of the underwater shore line. There are rocky caves, but nothing dangerous. The bottom is mostly gravel or basalt blocks,
which makes for good visibility under water. There are a
few spots where tall marsh grass grows near the shore, but
we can stay away from that."

"Boy, this sounds swell! I've never had the chance to
dive anywhere like this!" Fins's voice was eager, his face
alight with thinking about the fun just ahead.

"Well, don't be the eager-beaver type," Newt cautioned.
"Take it just as I say, and we'll go just as far with these
tests as you can go, but we'll try nothing you aren't ready
to try. Absolutely nothing. O.K.?"

Newt glanced at the boy beside him. Would there be
any trace of that stubbornness that he had seen on Fins's
face at the dock? If there was, he'd really make him take
it easy! The SCUBA Club had no place for stubborn brag-
garts.

But today Fins was not stubborn about anything. He
was in a listening and learning mood. Anything Newt
wanted him to do he would do or try to do ... and no
more. Newt was boss!

"O.K., Newt," Fins answered. "You call the plays."

"Fine! Well, here we are!"

They had turned off onto a road that was little more

than a trail. They rounded a short curve, and there was the lake, sparkling blue in the sun.

Although Fins would never have thought of it by himself, he could see why it was called a kettle lake. It was almost perfectly round and nestled there in the flat between the hills like a huge kettle filled with clear, clean water.

Near the far edge, a motorboat drifted along. Three men were in it. Two were fishing, while the other managed the boat.

"I'll put out a diving float," Newt said. "That will show the fishermen that there are divers over here. Most boatmen know what the red and white flag on a float means, and they stay away.

"Divers have no business around motorboats," Newt went on, "unless the boat is being used by the diving crew. The motor might start, the propeller start to whirl, and a diver could be finished off in a hurry. So just stay clear of motorboats."

Fins helped unload their gear. The heaviest was the rented lung.

They found a big rock which made a fine dressing room, and soon they were ready to dive—that is, except for the diving gear.

Newt showed Fins how to check the air in the lung.

"Now, we'll put our outfits on," Newt said. "Here's what the well-dressed skin diver will wear . . . or not wear! First, our neoprene suits. This lake water is too cold for any other kind. You put these on just as you would put on a two-piece suit of long underwear. Neoprene doesn't go on as easily as cloth, so we use a lot of this powder. That helps."

Fins watched every move that Newt made, and did just as he did. Getting that neoprene suit on did take time, but he did it.

He had an easy time with his fins. He had slipped into those so often. But the tank was another problem.

Fins put the straps where Newt told him to. Then he lifted the tank alone.

"I didn't know it would feel so heavy!" he panted, as he tried to get it on his shoulders in the right position.

"You're trying to put almost forty pounds on your back," Newt told him, "and it's dead weight in a metal case. So you're feeling every pound of it. But you'll get used to it, and the water will help you carry it. Now your mask and snorkel. I have a knife and depth gauge, so you won't need those today. Last comes the weight belt. Check it to make sure you can get it off fast if you have to. I'll take this length of shot rope, something every pair of divers should take."

When Fins was ready, Newt gave him a last check, and then he said, "First, we'll go down about ten feet. I'll go first. You follow. When we get down around ten feet, we'll level off, find a place to steady ourselves, and you remove the tank and put it back on under water. You're going to do that until you do it without a hitch. Then clear your mask. When you can do those two things, we will go down a little deeper. Be sure to keep your ears clear as we go down."

"I can do that," Fins said. "I've done it lots of times."

"You must be able to do it almost automatically, and often," Newt answered. "You don't want a popped eardrum. Ready?"

"Ready!" Fins replied, in a strong, happy voice.

Was he ready? He'd been waiting a long time for this moment.

Newt curved his body and rolled under the surface. Fins did the same thing and was under, and right at Newt's heels.

The water was almost as clear as a mirror. The warm surface water gave way to a layer several degrees colder.

A few lake trout swam lazily out from a rocky cove and followed them curiously. Fins reached out to touch the nearest fish, but he didn't make it. Suddenly he realized that everything looked closer than it really was. A rock seemed so close that it looked as if he might even kick it, but when he tried it he found that the rock wasn't even in touching distance.

The wonderful aloneness of the water held him like a magic spell. There was no noise except the bubbling of the lung, no trouble, nothing but quietness, friendly fish, the water, and the sun all mixing into shimmering beauty.

Down here, time wasn't important. It wasn't morning and it wasn't noon or night. He didn't even think about whether it was time for his paper-route work or not. The water was soft and easy, and without a meaning of time.

Newt didn't let him think long about the way he felt, for now he stopped on a rocky ledge and motioned Fins to remove his lung.

Fins knew just what he should do, but doing it wasn't so easy. He watched Newt's hands telling him what to do.

First, the weight belt must come off. He put it over his knee, just as Newt did.

"For if you don't," Newt had said, "you may start for the surface like a cork out of a bottle!"

Next, he unsnapped the straps holding his tank. Then a deep breath, take off the mouth piece, and slip out of the tank harness. It must all be done quickly, for that good breath of air wouldn't last very long.

Fins stood free of his tank.

Newt nodded his O.K., and Fins began to put the tank and belt back on. Then Newt motioned him to clear his mask and put it back. That was easy. Fins had often done that just on his own.

Although Fins knew he could remove his tank and put it back under water, he also knew he must do it again and again so he could do it very fast. There might come a time when he would have to leave the tank caught in a kelp jungle or wedged between rocks. He had read somewhere about things like that happening to skin divers. Not often, but a diver had to know what to do and how to do it . . . and fast . . . if it did happen.

He could tell that Newt was pleased with the way he had cleared his mask and put it back. But now he could see that Newt had another plan, for he was beckoning Fins to follow again.

Down, down, they went. The light was very strange, but still he could see quite well. Suddenly Newt leveled off and swam ahead. Fins followed.

I must be down fifty or sixty feet now, he thought. I don't think I've been down this far before.

Newt came near and gave him one end of the rope he had, and then went on ahead.

Big rocks rested on the lake bottom, the water breaking in little light shimmers around them. Here and there the water was dark, as if leading into a water cave.

And that's just what it was!

Newt led Fins into one of the dark places, so dark Fins couldn't see well. But he could feel the movement of the water between them, and the rope helped them keep near each other. Now Fins was very glad to have a good hold on that stout rope!

Suddenly they were out of the cave, and it was good to see the lightness of the open water.

Fins picked up a few rocks from the bottom. He wanted to see if the rocks were the same as some he had brought up from the river bed.

Newt made a motion for him to remove his tank again. It was much easier this time. He cleared his mask more quickly too.

When he got the tank on again, Newt made the motion that they would go up.

Fins remembered to exhale as he went up. He knew

this would keep the air from filling his lungs to the danger point. Exhaling wasn't really hard. It was just remembering that you had to do it.

They seemed to be coming up very slowly. But at last, they were on the surface, swimming toward shore.

Once more Fins was in the everyday world of earth people. Everyone with eyes to see could know what the earth was like, but only a few could know of that wonderful water world below.

And I'll know more than most skin divers, he thought, because I'm going to work at it. Wouldn't it be swell if I could be the best diver in the whole world? Wouldn't I like *that?*

5.

A STRANGE DIVING JOB

Fins and Newt cruised along on the surface toward the shore. The sun showed a mid-afternoon slant, and Fins knew it was almost time for his bundle of papers to come.

Newt seemed pleased with what Fins had done, but so far he hadn't said a word about his check-out score.

"Sure took us a long time to come up," Fins remarked.

Newt laughed. "I brought you up slowly," he said, "because you haven't been down that far before. When you go as far as one hundred feet down and stay there for awhile, you shouldn't come up faster than your slowest bubbles. So you may as well get used to taking your time. If you don't, you're just asking for a good case of bends.

"Underwater pressure is a queer thing. You can't feel it, unless you're wearing a dry suit, but it's there, more and more of it, as you go down. If you understand and learn to deal with it, you'll be O.K. As you go on with diving, you'll learn to handle different depths without even thinking about it."

They found their clothes behind the rock and were just

about to begin dressing when a loud scream cut the air. It came from the fishing boat.

"That boat's in trouble!" Newt exclaimed. "But what can it be? The boat is right side up, but all three men seem to be yelling for help. Come on! Won't take long to see what it's all about. Leave the lungs. They slow us down too much. But I'll take my shot line. It may come in handy."

Quickly they removed their tanks. Then they slipped into the water and swam smoothly, rapidly, toward the fishing boat.

As they came near enough to see the men, they saw a strange sight for a boat in trouble. Two men were laughing as if they could never stop, while the third was grinning in an embarrassed sort of way. It was plain that he didn't think the joke was as funny as the other two did.

When they had reached the boat, Newt said, "You guys don't look as if you needed to be rescued. What do you mean, sending out a false alarm like that?"

"It wasn't a false alarm," the driver of the boat said. "I'm Clem Andrews, and this is Jack Crandall, and this poor guy"—he nodded toward the man who had a hard time grinning—"he's Sam Colfax. He's a good guy, but right now he's got problems. He's almost toothless! Ha! Ha!" Clem Andrews laughed until he was nearly helpless from laughing.

Sam Colfax was getting angry.

"I don't think it's so funny!" he said, in a voice that sounded quite odd. "A man loses most of his teeth . . . store

teeth, yes ... but they do work ... and those guys think
it's funny. It's not funny! It's my upper plate, and it cost
me a lot of money. Now it's down there!" He pointed into
the depths of the water.

The one called Jack Crandall stopped laughing long
enough to explain what had happened.

"You see, Sam hasn't had this new dental plate very
long. It didn't fit very well, but he was getting by with it.
A fish took his bait, and he began pulling. The fish was
a good-sized fighter, and Sam got excited and did something with his tongue. That loosened the dental plate, and
it fell out into the water. We saw you fellows over there
diving and we thought you might be able to bring Sam's
teeth up for him."

"He lost the fish too," Clem said, with another fit of
laughing. "Only bite any of us got today, and old Sam lost
it! A fish and a new set of teeth lost in the same day's
work! Ha, ha!"

Fins looked straight at the man called Clem.

The effect on Clem was instantly quieting.

"Sure be good if you could get Sam's teeth for him," he
said. "We'd all chip in and pay you for it. We'll even pay
you for trying, whether you find the teeth or not."

"Never mind the pay," Newt said. "We'll try, but we
can't stay out here much longer. Fins has a paper route to
get back to, and I have things to do too. Besides, it won't
be easy to find anything as small as a dental plate, even
with water as clear as this. But here goes! Were you right
here when it happened?"

"Right here," Clem answered.

"O.K. Now, don't start that motor, not until we leave the job. Fins, you take this side, and I'll go to the other side. We can try for a few minutes."

Newt went to the other side of the boat and went under. Fins went down where he was.

The boat cast a shadow over them and made visibility good, once their eyes were used to the water.

Let's see, Fins was thinking, this guy would be excited about the fish. He'd be pulling back, reeling in his line, but he might lean over to play out the line so the fish would fight and tire out. However it happened, the teeth won't be too far from the boat. A dental plate isn't very heavy— anyway, I don't think it is—so the movement of the water could carry it out a little way as it was going down. So it won't be right under the boat. That is, I don't think it will.

The rocks were not very big in this part, and that would make it harder yet to find a dental plate. It could look so much like some of the rocks. And there were thousands of crevices just right for a small object to hide in.

Fins crawled around on the lake bottom, which, at this point, was only ten or twelve feet down. Several times he picked up rocks that looked like something else, but they were always just rocks.

Without a tank, he could stay under only a minute or so. The hunting was slow because of all his trips up for air.

In a few minutes Newt came around from the other side of the boat. He made a motion for them to surface.

When they reached top, Newt said, "I think this is hopeless. They think their boat is right where it was, but I'd be willing to bet it's several feet away from the exact spot, and that is as good as a mile when you're looking for something like a dental plate at the bottom of a lake."

"I know," Fins agreed. "But I would like to try once more. I'd like to circle around that boat, about ten feet out, and keep coming in closer and closer to it, always in a circle. Mel and I used to do that in the river, and lots of times we found what we were after that way. We only had a snorkel and mask, but we got along pretty well, if it wasn't too deep."

"Yes," said Newt, "you were doing a circle search. The big diving crews often do it that way when they are after something important, and small. It might work here, too, if we had time. O.K. We'll try it once that way. I'll use my shot line. We'll fasten that to the anchor on the bottom and take the line out about fifteen feet. I'll circle clockwise, and you go the other way. You can use the shot line. I'll do it without."

"O.K.," Fins agreed, and he turned for his dive.

Newt fastened the shot line to the anchor.

Fins took the free end and began his hunt. He circled under water as he had planned to do. He met Newt a couple of times.

He was crawling along the bottom at what he thought must be three or four feet away from the side of the boat when he saw a pile of rocks he hadn't noticed before. They were piled neatly, almost as if a child had started to make a rock fort at the bottom of the lake.

More curious than hopeful, Fins made for the rock pile. He began to pull the rocks apart and cast them aside. Suddenly he saw something that was quite a different color, wedged between a couple of the bigger rocks.

His lungs were begging for air. If he could only hold out a few seconds more! He'd never find this odd rock again if he left it now. He pulled desperately, and the strange little rock came loose.

Clutching the rock tightly in his hand, he went for the surface. Oh how wonderful that first gulp of air felt! He looked at the rock in his hand. Sure enough! Mr. Sam Colfax's new dental plate lay in his hand, grinning up at him.

Fins showed Newt his find.

"Good for you!" Newt exclaimed. "That was a good hunch you had about that second trip down. I would have been glad to call it a day. The whole thing looked so hopeless."

They trod water alongside of the boat and Fins said, "Is this what you wanted us to find, Mr. Colfax?"

He showed the men the dental plate, pink and wet in his hand.

"Boy, you're good!" Sam Colfax said happily. "I thought that was gone for good!" He pulled out his wallet and said, "Here, I'll trade you something for those teeth of mine. You can't use 'em anyway!"

Mr. Sam Colfax was beginning to see the joke now.

Fins looked at Newt. What would Newt want him to do?

Newt nodded. "Take it, Fins," he said. "That will help you buy the lung you want."

Fins traded the dental plate for the crinkly green twenty-dollar bill.

"Thanks," he said.

"Thank *you!*" Sam exclaimed.

"So long!" Newt said, "you'd better do something about that dental plate. There might not be any skin divers around the next time you lose it."

"I'll take care of it tomorrow!" Sam promised.

Newt took the shot line from the boat. He and Fins turned from the boat and swam back to their dressing room behind the big rocks.

As they were dressing and packing their gear, Newt said, "You're O.K., Fins. I give you a hundred per cent on your check-out! You can go anywhere we go now, as long as you remember the rules of SCUBA and live by them."

"Oh, I will!" Fins answered. He thought for a moment, and then he said, "I wasn't quite sure whether I ought to keep that money or not. I didn't know just how the club felt about such things. But I'm glad you let me keep it. Sure will be a big help on my savings for that lung."

"This is the way we feel about taking money for diving," Newt answered. "If the job is to save a life, or help the police, or help someone whom you know has very little money, then we just don't take pay. But this case was different. These men were out in an expensive fishing boat. I could see that they had all kinds of high-priced fishing gear. Their clothes were the best kind of sports clothes. Any of those men could give you twenty bucks and never miss it. Besides, if you hadn't found his dental plate, he would have paid much more than that for another one, and there'd be the unpleasantness of having it done."

When they got back to Fins's home, his papers were there, ready for folding.

Fins took his bike out of Newt's car and tossed his diving gear up on the lawn.

"Thanks a lot, Newt! Sure was swell of you to check me out today. See you at the meeting!"

"O.K.," Newt answered. "Better come to class next week. I'm going to show them how to do buddy breathing. That's one thing we didn't do today."

"Buddy breathing?" Fins asked, puzzled.

"Yes. Sharing the air in your tank with your buddy or using from his tank. It isn't hard to learn, but it's another thing a skin diver must be able to do quickly and well."

"All right, Newt," Fins answered, "if you say I should learn it, I'll get right at it. See you in class next week. So long!"

"So long!" Newt called, as he rolled off in his gay red car.

Fins watched the car as long as he could see it, busy with thoughts that went far ahead of the present moment. Maybe someday I'd like to teach swimming and diving. It would be great if I could get to be as good as he is and then teach other people. I wonder if I could . . .

6.

THE BOTTOM OF A RIVER

Fins saw Mel the next day, just before Mel went on duty at the city pool. They had a good laugh over the story of the teeth.

Mel said, "You know, Fins, I wouldn't be surprised to see you get to be a real big shot in this diving business someday."

Fins felt himself glow with importance.

"I hope you're right," he said, "but so could you, if you wanted to."

"I don't know," Mel answered. "I like diving, but not the same way you do, I guess. Besides, I want to go to school and get into some kind of science. But look . . . tomorrow is my day off. What say let's go out for a little diving on our own, just as we used to do?"

"Great!" Fins agreed. This would go along with the rules, for he would be with another diver. The diver didn't have to be a club member. It had been quite awhile since he'd been out with Mel, because this new job Mel had kept him pretty well tied down.

"Let's take our bikes and go to some part of the river

where people don't often come. Just beyond those old dredge hills might be pretty good," Mel suggested.

"O.K. Let's take a lunch and make a day of it!"

The dredge hills were big rocky hills and ridges made by miners many years ago when gold had first been found in the Mother Lode country. Men were greedy for gold, and when the easy gold had all been found, they began mining with machinery. After the ore was washed out, the leftover rock and dirt had been pushed over into big hills and mounds. Now the grass and some ragged shrubs were beginning to find roots in these man-made hills.

Mel and Fins had been around here before, but they hadn't done much diving in this part of the river. They did know that the river was quiet on the other side of the dredge hills, but it was hard to get over there, so few people ever went to that part to fish or swim.

They would swim and dive with the mask and snorkel, as they had often done.

When Fins got to Mel's home he said, "Let's take a pick and a heavy hammer. We might find something we want to break up."

"You going out for some wet mining?" Mel asked, laughing.

"Well, if we found a rock that looked good, it wouldn't hurt to break it up, would it? People do find gold trace in rocks sometimes."

"Oh sure! We have an old hammer and heavy pick around here somewhere."

Mel found the tools, and, with their lunches and diving gear strapped on behind, they had a load. It was hard to carry a heavy pick on a bike, so they took turns with the hammer and pick. But at last they reached the dredge hills.

Just as they thought. No one was here, and the river was quiet and bright in the sun. They found a cove where the water looked deep and clear. Clear, that is, for the American River. No part of it was ever like that little kettle lake up in the mountains.

The cove was quiet, and the water comfortably warm, but the boys couldn't see very well. It was like looking through a light fog. But for the American River it wasn't bad.

A few bass and small fish swam curiously around them. Fins never felt out of place with fish. They were his friends. Sometimes when he heard people talk about the dangerous fish of the deep waters he wondered how he would feel about them. Now, as he saw the bass almost close enough to touch, he thought, I wonder how it would be to get a close-up like that of a shark or a barracuda. And those moray eels! I've heard a lot of bad things about them. They must be the gangsters of the deep. Anyway, I'd like to call on those fellows sometime, right in their own back yards. Bet I will too!

But now he knew he was far away from shark waters. He was in the American River, near Sacramento, California, just swimming and diving here and there, looking for . . . well, most anything that might turn up.

He stepped on a slippery rock that seemed to be at the base of a lot of smaller rocks. Fins swam all around the place, poking at the rocks, pushing them around. Been a rock slide here once, he thought. I wonder why. No mountain steep enough to make a rock slide this big.

He picked up a rock. It seemed pretty heavy for its size. He made a signal to Mel that he was going up. Mel swam toward him. He, too, had a rock. Both boys started up.

They came to the surface and swam toward the river bank.

"Kind of a funny slide down there," Fins remarked.

"Yeah," Mel agreed. "Well, it's hard to tell what all happened here a thousand years ago. Someday I want to study things like that, and then I might know what to expect when I come on a big rock slide under water. Right now I can just guess."

"Guessing is fun, too," Fins said, "and not such hard work as studying to find out!"

Mel laughed. "You're still scared of school work, aren't you?"

"Darned right I am. It would be O.K. if a fellow could take what he wanted to find out about. But the good part is all mixed up with a batch of stuff most of us will never use."

"But how do we know we won't use it? My dad says he uses his bookkeeping courses all the time, and when he took bookkeeping he thought it was a complete waste of time."

Fins felt irritation rising in him. He didn't come out

here to argue about school. Mel had just better stop that
stuff or the whole day would be ruined!

"Lay off, Mel, will you? I don't want to think about
school. I came out here to swim and dive. I didn't come
to listen to a lecture."

"O.K.," Mel said. "Cool off! Let's go over ,and break
these rocks. See if we can find out why they are so heavy."

They found a rock shelf jutting out of the bank. Fins
put his small rock down and wham! went his hammer.

It took several hard blows to break the rock. There was
nothing inside but some streaks that looked as if they
might be rust.

Now Mel broke his. Inside was a greenish rock. He
broke that, and it shattered into a lot of tiny pieces. He
picked up a small, dirty chunk. It was very heavy. He
began scraping it with his knife.

Fins watched closely as Mel scraped. All at once both
boys gasped in surprise.

"Gold! That looks like gold, Mel—a little gold nugget!"
Fins exclaimed.

"Sure does!" Mel agreed. "I'll be darned!"

Now nothing could stop them. They had the gold fever,
a real case of it!

They dug a little hole near their clothes and put their
treasure in a handkerchief and laid the handkerchief in
the hole. They covered the hole with a couple of big, flat
rocks.

Before they went down again, Mel said, "You know,
I'll bet this is where an old mine caved in years and years

ago. It wasn't doing very well so no one tried to build it up again. I read about it somewhere."

"Oh boy! Let's be miners! What are we waiting for?" Fins asked. "Mine or not, we found it, and we may still get enough to pay us for our work. Maybe I can buy my lung with gold nuggets! Here goes!" He made a smooth surface dive and was gone.

Mel followed.

For a long time the boys worked on the rock pile. They used their snorkels for cruising just below the surface to locate the most promising rock formations. Then they took off the snorkels and went down in a free dive. Time after time they brought rocks to the surface, broke them up, and carefully examined the inside. Both boys found a few more very tiny bits of gold and several flakes. But the first one they found was the biggest.

At last the sun told them it was time to leave.

"Mel, let's come out here every day you have off," Fins sugested, "and let's not tell what we found here. We won't tell anyone!"

"Not even our family? I want to tell my folks, especially my dad. He can tell us where to sell this stuff. We might get into trouble if we try to get rid of it alone."

"O.K.," Fins said. "Tell your dad and mother, then, but nobody else."

Before Mel could answer, they heard a noise in the bushes a little way from where they were dressing. Voices came from the bushes—boy voices.

One said, "This might be as good a place as any. Nobody comes here. Anyway, not very often. The stuff won't have to be hidden very long."

Just then the boys came out of the bushes. The two from the bushes and the two boys on the rocks stared hard at each other. It was hard to tell which pair of boys was the most startled!

Fins spoke first.

"You're wrong about nobody coming here. Mel and I come here a lot . . . and look," he said to the taller boy, "I think I've seen you before."

The boy laughed an unpleasant, sneering laugh.

"A lot of guys look like me. That is, the cops think they do!" His steely blue eyes narrowed as he looked at the boy with him. He winked at his friend, but it was more of an evil squint than a wink. The two boys from the bushes laughed loudly. Whatever joke they had on the cops seemed to be very funny.

Fins felt a growing uneasiness inside. Somewhere he had seen that taller boy! Suddenly he remembered.

"Do you know Rich Morton?" he asked. "He comes to a skin-diving club I belong to. I think I've seen you with him. Not at the club, but on the street somewhere."

The tall boy hesitated. Then he said, "Sure, that must be where you saw me. I know Rich. Good diver, Rich is."

"Yeah," Fins agreed. He was still uneasy. This pair didn't seem like the kind of boys a SCUBA would run around with. But then, you couldn't know all the other friends your SCUBA pals would have. They didn't know about his friend, Mel, either.

"Well, I'm Fins Harper and this is my buddy, Mel Hanson. We swim and dive a lot and we come down here quite often."

Now the other boy spoke. He was a short, stocky boy who looked like a wrestler, or as if he would like to be one and had been working at it. His shifty black eyes roamed all over while Fins had been talking to his companion. Those eyes hadn't missed a thing: the diving gear, hammer, and pick, and the pounded rock.

Now he spoke.

"Well, how about *not* coming around here for awhile? There's a lot of places better than this for diving."

Fins didn't like the sound of that. Not one bit. No one could tell him where to swim and where not to. No one but Newt Browning, that is.

"Look, fellows, you haven't even told us your names."

Again came that hard, unpleasant laugh.

"Call us Shot Put and Hooker," said the short one. "Call me Shot Put, and he's Hooker!"

Fins knew very well those were not the boys' names, not even their nicknames. But he wouldn't argue with them about that.

"O.K.," he said, "Shot Put . . . and Hooker! This river is big. It's long, and in some places it's pretty wide. It curves a lot and in some spots it's deep. It's muddy and it's tricky. We know some of its tricks. But what I mean is . . . this is a big river, with a lot of room. We were here first and we know this is one of the best places around here for diving and rock hunting. I guess you could call us rock hounds. Well, anyway, we're going to come here as often as we want to and when we want to!"

The one who called himself Hooker shrugged.

"Just as you say. You might end up sorry, but that's your lookout, I guess."

Mel and Fins glared at the newcomers, and they glared right back. Fins wanted to leave, for it was almost time for his paper route. But he wouldn't leave what they had put under the two big flat rocks. He couldn't leave Mel alone with these two roughers, and somebody had to stay until they could get their gold.

But in a few minutes Shot Put was tired of the glare system. He nudged Hooker and said, "C'm on. We're not gonna do any more today anyway. We got things to do other places. These jokers probably won't come back."

With one last parting glare, the two turned back into the bushes, and Mel and Fins could hear them making their noisy way through the undergrowth along the river bank.

"H'm, pleasant characters," Mel said.

"They haven't scared me any," Fins declared. "I'm coming back here when I please and as often as I want to come. How about you?"

"I'll come along," Mel said. "But look, Fins, don't come here alone. Those guys have been around. They would just as soon pound us into jelly as not, if we got in their way.

They would be afraid to tackle both of us, I think, but one would be duck soup for them."

"I guess you're right," Fins admitted. "Anyway, a rule of the club is that we never dive alone, so I'll wait until you come too. How about your next day off?"

"Fine! We'll come back here next Thursday then."

They picked up their diving gear, their small gold treasure, packed everything on their bikes, and pushed their loads up the bank. Then they headed for the road back to town and home.

As they rode along toward home, they talked about the strange boys who wanted to be boss of the river. Who were those boys? What were they up to? Why did they want that special part of the river? They didn't seem to be divers, and they didn't seem interested in the rocks around there.

What *did* they want?

Right now the boys could only guess, and they knew their guesses were wild, very wild.

7.

STRANGERS AT THE RIVER

That night Fins told his mother what had happened at the river.

"Hooker and Shot Put don't sound like the kind of boys you should get mixed up with," she said.

"I won't get mixed up with 'em, Mom," he promised. "They sure don't appeal to me."

"By the way," his mother said curiously, "I wonder what they *do* plan to do down there? Why should they care if other people come there to swim or fish?"

Before Fins could answer, his mother thought of something else.

"How did you get along with that swimming teacher from the Y the other day? Did you check out on diving O.K.?"

Fins could almost feel his mother holding her breath, waiting for his answer. He looked at her quickly, and straight. This was the first time she had shown any real interest in his diving activities. Could she be softening up a little about it?

He told her what Newt had said.

"I still have to learn to do buddy breathing."

He explained it as Newt had done with him.

"Sounds like an odd way to breathe," his mother remarked.

"I guess you can't be choosy under water, if you get low on air. Newt wants me to take that class he's giving. I don't really need anything but this first lesson on buddy breathing; it will only take one night a week and it will cost me the rent on a tank. That won't be much. I might pick up a little know-how that I don't have, and it will be fun to be with other people who like to play around down under."

Mrs. Harper shivered.

"What a way to spend a good free evening!"

But this time she didn't argue with Fins about the danger.

On Wednesday night he went to the Y and got into the diving class. What fun it was to dive around with people just as water-crazy as himself!

Once when he was coming up to rest, he saw Bob and Betsy coming toward him. A younger girl was with them, a thin little creature with a shy, pleasant face.

"This is my little sister, Mary," Betsy said. "She's a real good swimmer, but she's just beginning lung diving. I thought you might like to meet someone your own age."

"Sure," Fins answered. "Hi!" There didn't seem to be much else to say.

Mary said Hi! in a shy little voice, and that was all.

H'm! She wasn't loaded with words, either.

Just then Newt called the group together.

"Tonight we will work on buddy breathing," he said.

He explained why it was so important to do it well. Then he counted them off to work in pairs. Fins found himself counted off with Mary!

What a thing to happen to a fellow!

No one else seemed to think it was strange, so he began to feel better about it too.

Mary got her tank on and it was almost as big as she was! But she handled it well.

"Have you done any tank diving yet?" he asked.

"Oh yes, a few times, but I'm not very good at it. My family won't let me dive anywhere but in the pool. That's O.K. I have lots of fun here."

Newt showed them all how to handle their outfits for buddy breathing. Then he had each pair of divers do it for practice. Everyone got along fine, even Fins, who had never done it before.

Under water, they took turns doing buddy breathing until they could do it smoothly. When the other divers began going to the surface Fins and Mary went up too.

Suddenly Fins realized he was thinking of Mary as just any other diver, instead of a funny little girl with big brown eyes that looked shy most of the time.

That night was the beginning of six wonderful sessions at the pool. Each time he learned something new about diving or taking care of his gear, or planning for a big dive. Always he felt himself gaining skill with the lung.

On Mel's free day the two boys often went to the river. They found a few flakes of gold each time but no big finds. Once they found signs that their rock slide and diving spot had been visited by others. The underwater rock slide was scattered as if someone had used a dynamite charge on it.

On their first trip down that day they found a big thing covered with rust and mud and tangled tree roots. It was hard work to bring it up, for the thing was heavy. They had to make several tries at it because they had to go up for air so often. But at last the thing lay, wet and slimy and shapeless, on the river bank.

"What do you think it is?" Fins asked. "Maybe we just brought up an old tree root with odd-looking side arms!"

Mel poked it with his pick, and then he said, "You know, I think this is an old, old mining tool. Maybe a pick or something. Won't take too long to find out."

Mel was right. When they had cleaned off the mud and tangled roots, they had a miner's pick, rusty and useless for mining, but an interesting old piece.

"I know somebody who would like to have this, I'll bet," Mel said.

"Who in the world would want a thing like this?" Fins asked. "I think we just wasted our time. I'm tired. That was hard work!"

"I'm tired too. But you know, I think the State Museum in Sacramento would like to have this. We'll take it and find out."

"Well, they can have it!" Fins exclaimed.

Fins would have left the old pick right there on the river bank, but Mel talked him out of it. Mel rattled on about the history of mining tools until Fins found he was getting interested in spite of himself.

"Where do you find out all this stuff?" Fins asked.

"I got interested in the Mother Lode country when our history class studied the westward movement, so I got extra books from the library. You oughta check out some of those. They're good stuff."

Fins grunted, but he didn't make a sensible answer. Libraries made him think of school, and school was what he didn't want to think about.

Mel didn't even notice Fins's lack of interest in the Mother Lode books. He went on talking about finding the old miner's pick.

"And if it hadn't been for someone breaking up that rock slide, we would never have found it! I wonder who did that?" Mel asked himself and Fins.

"I think I can tell you, in one guess," Fins answered. "I think Shot Put and Hooker did it. They've been checking up to see if we're still coming here, and they know we do. So they broke up the rock slide to spoil things for us. They are too dumb to know they helped us!"

"Well, thank you, Hooker! Thanks, Shot Put!" Mel said, with mock politeness. "Come on, Fins, let's get this thing to my house. My dad will help us get it to the museum."

They put their diving gear and tools on one bike and the heavy old pick on the other. Then they took turns on the bikes so one boy wouldn't have the same load all the time.

It was a hard pull, but at last they reached Mel's home.

Mr. Hanson was more excited than the boys about their find. "I'm going to call the museum director right away!" he said.

When he came back from the phone he said, "The director wants me to bring the pick, and you boys, to the museum tonight. Can you go, Fins?"

"Sure," Fins answered. This thing was beginning to look important, and he liked important things.

When he told his mother about their find, he got the surprise of his life.

"Would you take me over to Mel's house after supper?" he asked. "Mr. Hanson wants to take us and this old pick to the museum."

"Sure," she answered quickly, so quickly that Fins almost fell out of his chair with surprise. But his mother had another surprise for him.

"How about taking me to the museum with you? I think it would be sort of fun."

"Why—why, sure. I just thought you wouldn't be interested," he said. What had come over his mother lately?

She answered his unspoken question.

"If you are so set on this diving business, maybe I'd better get used to it. I'm still not real happy about it, though," she warned.

"Gee, Mom! Just to have you this much interested is the best news I've heard for a long time. You know something? Maybe I'll get you down in a SCUBA rig someday!"

Margaret Harper shook her head firmly. She knew she would never go down in any kind of a diving rig any time. It was bad enough to say that she would try to get used to it because Fins liked it so much. But that was as far as she would go . . . ever!

8.

PICTURES IN THE PAPER

Mr. Jacobs, head of the museum, was waiting for them. He looked at the old mining pick closely, then he said, "It's one of the old forty-niner picks, all right. It's a pretty good one too. Must have been almost new when the miner lost it, or the mine caved in on it, or whatever happened. We'll put it in the room with other Western things. But first, we want a picture of you fellows with the pick. You're presenting it to the museum, see? You don't mind, do you?"

The boys looked at each other in surprise.

Pictures? In the paper, maybe, just for diving down and finding an old rusty mining pick? Oh boy!

The photographer already had things set up for the picture. He took three shots, and that was it.

"Now," said Mr. Jacobs, "I want to know a few things about this find. How deep was it? Did you know it was a pick when you saw it down there?"

He asked other questions, and the boys answered as best they could.

"The museum has no money to pay for things like this,"

Mr. Jacobs said. "But the story will be in the paper tomorrow and you may get a few little diving jobs because of that."

"We don't do these things for pay, Mr. Jacobs," Fins said. "It's just fun to see what goes on down there. Someday I want to make my living as a skin diver, but right now we do it for sport."

"You'll need a pretty good education to get a steady job in skin diving," Mr. Jacobs said, "but boys as smart as you two seem to be won't have any trouble in school."

Fins felt himself getting angry. The very thought of school did this to him, always!

"I'll bet there will be jobs I can do and good ones, too, without a lot of stupid schoolwork," he said. "I've quit school and I'm not going back!"

Mr. Jacobs looked beyond Fins at his mother.

Mrs. Harper said nothing. She gave a little shrug as if to say, "Well, that's the way it is!"

Mr. Jacobs looked back at Fins again.

"You might be right," he said. "I'm just telling you what I know about the best jobs for divers, like working with crews that test for oil under water, bridge crews that plan the underwater framework of the big bridges—and oh, all kinds of things! But as you say, there may be others that don't take much schoolwork."

After a little talk about Mel's plans and some more pleasant visiting, Mel's father took them home.

The only thing that left a bad feeling with Fins was remembering how Mr. Jacobs had looked when Fins had said he wasn't going on to school.

Oh well, he thought, I mustn't let that kind of stuff bother me. It will happen as long as I still look like a school kid. But just wait until I'm grown up. Just wait!

When the paper came out next day—sure enough—there was the story! It wasn't on the front page, but it was with the local news in the middle.

Fins's mother looked a long time at that picture, but she said nothing.

Fins cut the picture out and put it up in his room. He liked that picture. It was fun to do things that other people thought were important enough to be in the paper, with a picture! But I'll do a lot more than this, he said to himself. This is just the beginning!

9.

HOW ABOUT RICH MORTON?

Mr. Jacobs was right about the jobs that came because of the story in the paper.

Fins and Mel went together on the first call, with Fins using a rented tank and Mel ready for free diving.

They found a motor that had come loose from the boat and had gone down about ten feet. That wasn't a very hard job, and the owner paid them well for their work.

The jobs that came after that all had to be done by lung divers. Fins got someone from the club to help him on those. He and a club friend found a wrist watch that had been dropped overboard. They brought up a good camera with a broken strap. It had fallen from the owner's shoulder, but, since it was in a waterproof case, it wasn't hurt at all.

Fins and Rich cleaned one of the houseboats in the harbor. It was a messy job, but it paid well. It gave Fins a chance to talk to Rich about Hooker and Shot Put.

"Saw some friends of yours at the river," he remarked.

"Yeah? Who?"

"They called themselves Hooker and Shot Put."

Rich laughed.

"Oh, those guys! I just know who they are, and that's about all."

Fins tried to find out more about Shot Put and Hooker, but Rich clammed up. He wasn't saying another word.

Then Fins turned the conversation to Rich himself. For some strange reason, this boy, two years or more older than he, aroused his curiosity. He was not the type who would usually be going around with young thugs such as Hooker and Shot Put seemed to be. Still, he always had an attitude of being easy toward the world in general. He knew about a lot of things Fins had never heard of; perhaps that was the pull Fins felt, for he was curious about everything, especially everything about the water and diving.

"Do you go to school here in town?" Fins asked.

"Nope. Quit in my junior year."

"Sorry you quit?" Fins asked.

"Nope . . . I guess not." Suddenly Rich's voice took on a tone of anger. "What is this? Some kind of third degree?"

"Forget it," Fins answered. "I just quit school myself."

When the boat-cleaning job was done, they went their separate ways. Fins was more curious than ever about Rich Morton.

Fins and Mel didn't go to the river again. Mel was busy with his job, and Fins was busy with his paper route and the diving jobs that kept coming up. Once a week he went in for the skin-diving class.

Just a few days before his fourth lesson, he counted his savings again. Mel's father had helped them sell their gold flakes, and that, with his paper money and his diving jobs, had built his savings up pretty fast.

While he was figuring with his bankbook and pencil, he suddenly felt so happy he could have yelled all over town. But he didn't. He only screamed so loudly that his mother almost fell off the sofa.

"What in the world hit you?" she asked, startled.

"I have enough—a little more than enough!" he shouted.

"Enough of what? For what?" she asked.

"Enough dough for my lung," he said. "I know just the one I want. I've been seeing it every night on my route. Tomorrow I'll get it. Boy, oh boy!"

Mrs. Harper sank down with a sigh. Nothing would keep that boy on top of the water now, or out of it, she thought.

When Fins went for his lesson next day, it was a real high-spot time, for now he had his own lung. No more rented ones. He had the dream of his whole swimming life —a bright new lung, painted yellow so it could be seen a long way under water. It was the latest thing for safety and easy handling.

Bob and Betsy and Mary stopped for him that night, because he couldn't carry a thing like that on his bike.

"Boy, what a lung! That one will take you any place a skin diver has any business going!" Bob said admiringly. "It has the best regulator you can get."

Bob's admiration was only the beginning of what happened that night. For Fins found himself the center of attention at the pool.

When the class was over, Newt had some big news for them.

"This weekend some of us are going ocean diving," he said. "We're going to Carmel. Some of you know what it's like to dive there."

"That's great!" Rich exclaimed. "Best diving this side of Catalina."

"What's it like?" Fins asked.

"Water so clear you can count the pebbles on the bottom," Rich answered. "I picked up some cool dough there last summer, just diving for coins the tourists threw into the water."

"That will be great!" said Fins. "I've never done any ocean diving. Is it hard?"

"Not so hard, but different," Rich answered. "Newt will send someone with you who has done ocean diving several times," Rich said.

"Fine! How about you and me going buddies? You know the tricks of the ocean."

Rich said nothing, and just as Fins was beginning to think Rich hadn't heard him, Newt dismissed the class. Fins turned to repeat his question, but Rich was gone. He was already out of his gear and headed for the dressing room.

Why is he in such a hurry? Fins asked himself.

Before he could follow Rich, Mary was asking him

something. He hardly answered her, because he was still thinking about Rich.

"Just a minute, Mary. I gotta catch Rich!"

Rich had already left the dressing room.

"He seemed in an awful hurry," one of the men said.

Fins got out of his gear and dressed as fast as he could. Now it seemed very important to find Rich.

At last he was outside, looking for Rich.

Suddenly he saw him, standing by a souped-up car, talking to a couple of boys. Fins started for the car.

"Rich!" he called. "Rich, I want to see you!"

But Rich didn't answer. He was talking to the boy at the wheel of the souped-up car. Then the boy turned his head and saw Fins.

All of a sudden the boy stepped on the gas and the car leaped forward into the night, but not before Fins had seen the driver.

For there behind the wheel, sending the car wildly forward into the darkness, was the face of a boy Fins would never forget—the boy who called himself Hooker!

10.

ON TO THE SEA!

Saturday morning came at last, the beginning of a big weekend of ocean diving. Fins had almost counted the hours since class night on Wednesday. Today he would be doing a kind of diving he had only read and heard about.

This was one morning when he didn't need a second call to get up! Long before it was time to leave, he was ready. He took camping things, too, for they would stay until late the next day.

When Newt's car pulled up in front of the house, Fins wanted to yell for joy. This was the end of the waiting!

Two other carloads of club members pulled in behind Newt.

Mrs. Harper came out to see them off.

"Mother," said Fins, "I want you to meet Newt Browning. He's the swimming and diving teacher at the Y—the guy I've been telling you about."

Mrs. Harper looked at Newt in a sizing-up way.

Fins watched closely. If only his mother could see Newt as he, Fins, saw him, then she would be glad to have him with Newt, even if it did mean more swimming and diving.

Now his mother spoke, in a very matter-of-fact way.

"I'm glad to meet you, Mr. Browning. I hope you're a careful diver. Some aren't. Frank talks about you most of the time. I have you served up with every meal I have at home!"

"How awful!" Newt answered, laughing. "You have a very good diver here, Mrs. Harper. I think he'll do some pretty important work in diving someday."

"Oh, I hope not!" Mrs. Harper exclaimed. "I hope it's just something he'll get over, like kids get over the measles! If I can only keep from blowing up too many times while he's getting over it!"

"Come down to the Y sometime and watch my classes," Newt invited. "Skin diving is safe, if you learn the right way and stick to the rules. That's true of any sport."

Before Mrs. Harper could answer, two more loads of SCUBA people arrived.

"Well, I guess we're all here," Newt said, as he checked his group. "Rich called and said he couldn't make it today. I'm sorry about that, for I was going to team him up with Fins. Rich is good at ocean diving. He knows the surf so well."

"Did he say why he couldn't come?" Fins asked.

"No," Newt answered. "Just that something came up. Rich is like that. He's a top-notch diver, but he seems to have a lot of outside interests besides diving. Oh well, we'll get along."

Newt helped Fins get his gear into the car, and they were off.

In the back of his mind, Fins kept thinking about Rich. Did Hooker have something to do with Rich staying home from this trip? It must be pretty important to Rich, for Rich had told him a lot about ocean diving. He seemed to like it more than any other kind. Why, then, did he miss the first ocean trip of the season?

But Fins didn't intend to think about Rich all day.

For a few minutes they rolled along, saying nothing, just enjoying the clear morning air, listening to the purr of the little sports car as it ate up the miles.

Newt began telling Fins about the plans for the week-end.

"You're going to see a lot of skin-diving fun this trip," he said. "Some of the fellows are going spear fishing. I used to do a lot of that, but I'd rather hunt with a camera. I have my underwater camera things along, and I hope to get some good shots. Some of the gang want to get up early in the morning and go ab hunting. Bob, Betsy, and Mary will be in that bunch."

"Ab hunting?" Fins asked, puzzled.

"Abalone," Newt answered. "You have to dive free for that. It's against the law to use a lung in most places. You know about abalone, that big shellfish that sticks to a rock and has to be pried off with an iron and sometimes a lot of strength. After you get the trick of it, you can do it with your hands."

"That sounds like great sport!" Fins exclaimed.

"There will be fellows out ab hunting for fish companies," Newt went on. "They are helmet divers, and they have to go down twenty feet or more. That's the law. Abs aren't found much deeper than forty feet, so you will see the fish companies working out from shore in the twenty- to forty-foot water. They have no limit on numbers, but they must watch size, just as the sport hunters do.

"People like our SCUBA crowd may hunt abs near the shore, but we may take only five per person each day, and they must be at least seven inches across. If everyone keeps to his limit and watches the rule on size, we can have ab fishing as a sport for a long time. If many people go over the limit, the abs near the shore will soon be gone. Then all ab hunters will have to go out in the deep and fight it out with the commercial fishermen.

"We'll go out a little way and drop down ten or fifteen feet to a rocky shelf Bob and I know about. Then you won't have to work against those fellows who do it every day for a living."

"Sounds like you do a lot of ocean diving," Fins remarked, "or you wouldn't know where these rocky shelves are."

"Well, that's a know-how you pick up two ways . . . no, three ways," Newt answered. "First, by diving and finding out. Submarine crews and deep-sea divers have learned a lot about what lies under the water. Second, you read about diving, everything you can find. Third, you listen to other people who have gone down.

"There's so much yet to learn about the world down under. We've only begun to find out about it. The big colleges are sending out diving crews to study life away down. Oil companies and other big industries are sending out crews to test for oil and other minerals in the water or under the ocean's floor. Engineering teams hire divers to make maps of rocks under water in places where they want to build a bridge or dam. There are dozens of ways that good skin divers can be very useful."

"That's what I want to do . . . get a big diving job when I'm grown up, maybe my own crew," Fins said excitedly. "What fun it'll be! Do you think I can?"

"I'm sure you'll be able, as a diver, to do it," Newt answered.

There was something about the way Newt put his answer that made Fins uneasy.

"What do you mean . . . that I'd be able as a diver to do it? What else would be in the way?"

"I don't think you'd be interested in the other angles of it," Newt replied. Suddenly he pointed to the coastal range they were about to enter.

"See those hills?" Newt asked. "They aren't big hills at all, but really they are part of a mountain chain that goes on down into the ocean. About five or six hundred feet down there is a sharp drop, something like a high mountain ledge. This is called the continental shelf. There's more land under water than there is above it. Did you know that?"

Fins shook his head.

"I'd sure like to go down to that continental shelf," Newt went on. "Some people say that most plant and animal life of the sea live on the continental shelf. It's sort of like the grazing lands of some parts of the country. Meadows of the deep, I guess you'd call it. But it's just too far down for skin diving. Some of us are going to a shore reef about five miles out. We'll go down around a hundred to a hundred and twenty-five feet, but we can't stay long. I hope to get some good camera shots of sea life down there."

"Can't I go with you?" Fins asked. "Don't you think I could take a deep dive now?"

Newt was quick with his answer.

"No," he said. "For you that would be too much of a chance. You'll have to do a lot of ocean diving first. After you've had a taste of that, you'll know why you can't go out with me on this trip. You'll have fun with the bunch that wants to go ab hunting in the morning."

For a moment Fins had forgotten the ab-hunting trip.

"Sure," he said, "I guess I can't do everything at once."

During the rest of the trip, they talked of many things. Fins found that Newt had been almost everywhere that skin divers go. Hearing him tell about it was like listening to a wonderfully exciting story.

In those stories, Newt took him from the sponge and coral divers of the South Pacific seas to the oyster beds of the Atlantic Coast. He told him about the sunken treasures of the world, some of which would never be found.

"Now, that's something else I'd like to do!" Fins said. "Gee, it would be fun to dive away down under and bring up an old sea chest filled with pirate's gold!"

Newt laughed. "You've been reading comic books," he

said. "Yes, that's what a lot of people think, but that isn't the way it goes with sea treasure."

Fins looked at him with questions in his eyes.

"You see," his friend continued, "there are big companies called salvage companies that make a business of sending diving crews down where ships have been known to sink. Whatever they bring up belongs to the company and the country where the ship came from. Laws between nations deal with undersea wrecks. You could be in real trouble if you found sunken treasure and tried to bring it up yourself.

"And even if the laws would let you do it, sunken treasure ships aren't the easiest things in the world, or under it, to find. Many are on shallow reefs, but so covered with silt, slime, and old sea litter that they are hard to recognize.

"Some of the lost ships may have gone away down into the abyss of the ocean, and that's the same as a car rolling down into the crack in a glacier or down to the bottom of one of the deepest canyons of the great Grand Canyon. Only, besides being deeper than we can even measure in some places, the ocean's abyss is filled with water. So I think sunken treasure is out for most of us, but it's fun to think about."

"Yeah," Fins agreed, "I think I'll be diving just for fun for a few years, anyway."

"That's the best way to really enjoy it," Newt answered. "Don't expect the sea to give you anything. Then when you get something from its depths, it's a wonderful surprise!"

By this time they could see the blue water of the Pacific, stretching out beyond the reach of their eyes. The blue sparkled in the morning sun, the rolling surf from out at sea came in gently and broke into easy little cotton-topped waves that lapped at the rocks and the sandy beach.

Newt followed a road down to a camp near the shore. He stopped his car near a campsite.

"Well, this is it," he said.

Fins said nothing. He was too busy breathing in the good air from the sea, too busy watching the white gulls dipping their wings over the water.

The other cars came, and things began to happen. The air was filled with gay laughing and chattering of people out for fun and sport. Everyone seemed to know what to do to set up camp. They went about doing it quickly, but not quietly!

"We'll feed you fellows now," Betsy said, "but we expect you to bring in your own meat for supper!"

"How about a slinky octopus served up with all his eight arms in cream sauce?" asked Hank.

"You bring an octopus and you can cook it!" Betsy answered.

"Or a nice shark steak!" another said.

"Will we find sharks here?" Fins asked. "Real, man-eating sharks?"

"I hope not!" Newt exclaimed.

"Sharks are generally creatures of the deeper waters, but they do sometimes come up close to shore. There aren't any this far north, and they aren't as dangerous as news stories want us to believe. But all the same, a shark must kill to live, and I don't go around where they are if I can help it. People in the SCUBA Club know they should avoid splashing and quick movements when they go diving in the deep waters. Activity attracts the murderers of the sea. And if you get a little scratch, come to shore and take care of it. Sharks and barracudas have a sharp nose for blood. If they smell blood, they move in for the kill, and they don't care whether it's man or fish. Blood means food, and that's what they'd be after."

"Ugh!" Mary said, shuddering. "Don't talk about sharks!"

"Well, sweetie, you're not going out there anyway," her sister said. "You're going to dive in the nice, quiet coves, you know."

"Sure," Mary answered. "I don't want to dive anyplace else."

"Why don't you kids go down and see if you can find some sea urchins?" Newt suggested. "They're interesting little creatures. Be on the lookout for a good place to take off on the ab hunt in the morning too."

Fins and Mary walked along, looking down into the quiet little pools of clear water between the rocks, watching for the queer, spiny little round creatures called sea urchins.

"Did you ever see any?" Mary asked.

"No, but I've seen pictures of them. I think I'd know one if I saw it."

They kept on walking, going around one cliff and another, until they could no longer hear the noise at the

campsite. They were about to turn and go back, when, suddenly, Mary saw a tiny sea urchin at the base of a flat rock. They walked on, and found others.

"Sea urchins are thick here," Mary said. "This looks like a good place for ab hunting too. Let's mark this cliff."

They put a pile of small rocks on top of the cliff to mark the place. Just as they started to climb down, a loud yell cut the breeze.

They stopped short, clung to the rocks, and listened. Shrill and fear-laden, it came again.

"That's a call for help!" Fins exclaimed. He went down the cliff as fast as he could, Mary close behind him.

Off in a cove a man waved his arms madly, calling "Help! Help!"

Fins and Mary ran as hard as they could to the screaming swimmer.

"Got my leg caught!" he shouted. "Rock slid over and pinned me in. I can't move the rock *or* my leg!"

Fins kicked off his shoes and plunged into the water.

It wasn't hard to get to the man, but he was in real trouble. Fins couldn't move the rock, either.

He yelled back at Mary, "Get Newt, quick! The tide's coming in, and it's gonna go over his head if we don't get him out of here . . . fast!"

Without questioning, Mary ran back toward camp. Soon she was out of sight. Now he could only wait and hope for time.

But in a few minutes Newt and Bob were running like a couple of trackmen along the beach toward him.

Good thing they're fast, Fins thought. That tide is coming in. It isn't waiting for anything!

Quickly Fins told Newt the trouble.

"Come on, Bob!" Newt said. "I think all three of us can move that rock."

One big push, with all three pushing hard at the same time, and the rock moved. Not much, but enough for the man to move his leg and get out.

The man was not hurt, but he was exhausted from trying to get himself out, and from fear. Newt helped him to shore and then helped him get his tank off.

"Where are your friends?" Newt asked. "Don't you know a diver should never go out alone? Here you are, using a scuba rig, all by yourself!"

"I had work to do," the man said, with a grunt. "I wanted to work alone."

"Where's your car?" Newt asked. "Or your camp?"

"Camp is over there." The man pointed. "Don't need to take me there. I can make it. Thanks for comin' when you did!"

"I don't like to let you go like this," Newt said. "You just about got yours, and I don't think you should be alone for awhile."

Then the man became ugly and bad-tempered.

"Let me alone, I tell you! You saved my life. O.K. Thanks a lot, but that doesn't mean you gotta baby-sit me now. Go on back to your own camp."

Before Newt could answer, Bob came sloshing through the water, Fins just behind him, carrying something.

Fins held the thing out toward the man.

"This yours?" he asked.

"An ab iron!" Newt exclaimed. "So that's why you wanted to work alone. You used scuba gear for ab hunting, and you know that's against the law. So you probably have a lot more than your day's limit."

The stranger sat on the sand, sullen and not talking.

"Come on," Newt said quietly, "take us over to that ab catch you have. We'll help you toss them back into the sea, all but the five you are allowed to catch."

The stranger looked at the three strong young men standing over him. He shrugged. He walked slowly to his catch, with Fins, Newt, and Bob following.

Fins looked at the big stack of shellfish.

"Gee whiz!" he said. "Looks like fifty anyway!"

"Get those abs back in the canvas bags and we'll take them out to the rocks where they belong," Newt ordered.

The man did as he was told, with Bob and Fins helping. They left five big ones, which were all he was supposed to have.

"Next time go ab hunting the way you should," Newt said, "and you won't be getting into tight spots. And quit when you get five!"

"I suppose you'll turn me in for this," the man remarked in a low, but angry, voice.

"Not this time," Newt said, "but I am taking your car license number and, whenever I see this car on any beach,

I'll be looking for a guy who doesn't know the fishing laws of his state!"

Bob and Fins swam out to the rocks and dumped the abs. Then they started back to camp with Newt, leaving the man standing by his five abs.

"Not very happy about having his life saved, was he?" Fins asked.

"All that guy can think of is the fact that he got caught. Maybe we should have tossed him back in the sea!" Bob said.

"Well, he knows we won't do that," Newt answered. "Hey, I think I smell hamburger. Come on, let's race for it!"

Some of the girls came out to meet them, anxious to hear the story of the rescue. The three heroes took turns telling about it, shoving hamburger and buns into their mouths between times.

"Boy, what a good start on a real fun weekend!" Fins said.

"Well, let's hope we don't have to fish out any more drowning law-breakers! I'd a lot rather dive for fun!" Newt answered.

While they rested, they talked about the afternoon's plans. Today there would be one dive through the surf, and that was all.

"But first we're going to get over this picnic," Newt said.

So, stretched out on the beach like a bunch of lazy sand dollars, they did just that. Once more the campsite by the sea was quiet.

11.

BEYOND THE SURF

It was good to rest after a big picnic dinner, but Fins could hardly wait until Newt should give the word for a dive.

At last that word came.

"O.K.!" Newt called. "All you lazy clams wake up now!"

Fins was the first to have his gear ready. His whole body tingled at the thought of getting into that rolling surf, and then beyond it. He knew it might be hard, but he liked hard things like this.

"I'm taking Fins through the surf myself," Newt said. "I guess he is the only one who has never had any ocean diving—that is, where you have to go through the surf, except our little Mary, and she isn't going into it for a year or two. Anyone else want to go with us?"

Two divers whom Fins didn't know very well wanted to go. They got their gear and began to put it on. As they worked, Newt told them about getting into and through the surf.

"This is a calm sea," he remarked. "I've been watching the roll of the breakers.

"I think the best place to get into the surf is over between those rock ledges. The water is calm there, and we
can be almost at diving depth before we get to the breaker
front. Now we each have a float. We walk out into the
water until we're deep enough to float. Then we ride high
on the float and beyond the breaker front as it comes near
the shore line. We will find the water pretty quiet between the breakers. Quiet, that is, for the ocean. There is
always lots of movement in the sea. You'll find it's different from pool, or lake, or river diving. Some people even
get seasick from ocean diving."

Fins laughed. "That sounds funny! A diver getting seasick!" he said.

"Well, they do, sometimes, and if it happens, it isn't
funny. I don't think you will have any trouble, however.
But you will feel movement up and down and back and
forth. The sea is restless, and you will be right in the
middle of all this moving. But just let yourself go with
it, learn to understand it, and you'll be O.K. All set?"

Newt made a last quick check of all divers and their
gear.

"Here we go!" he called.

Fins followed Newt, trying hard to go just where he
went. Fins knew it the moment they were out of the shore
water. He would never forget the way he felt when that
first great roll of water hit them.

"Roll with the float and kick!" Newt yelled.

Fins kicked . . . he kicked like mad! Now he was through

that big breaker front, and in this wonderful, moving, swelling sea. What fun!

Fins had been to the seashore on picnics, and he had done his share of paddling around in the water near the shore. He had even been out far enough that he could stand and let the small breakers hit him. But he had never gone out beyond the breaker front like this. He knew it wasn't safe unless you could swim very well, and dive almost as well.

But now he felt safe, for he knew he was at home in the water, and he was following the lead of a man who had done this many, many times, and who knew exactly what to do and how to do it.

Some of the SCUBA fellows were in a boat they had brought along. The boat followed the bubbles and floats of the skin divers. That little boat gave Fins a feeling of safety, too, although they didn't need to use it.

Newt put Fins through several kinds of diving stunts. They found a mass of kelp and worked their way through it. How funny it looked, like a big tent over them.

Newt showed him how to spread it apart and work through it. It would be bad if a fellow got scared in a thing like this, Fins thought. But if you don't get scared and you know what to do, there isn't a thing to worry about.

Their deepest down point was fifty feet, and they stayed only a few minutes there. Then Newt made the sign for an easy coming up. They were out in the surf about an hour, which Newt said was plenty for the first time.

They came out of the sea just as they had gone in, watching the surf for the low point, then floating and kicking through the breaker front until they got to walking depth.

"Well," said Newt, when they were in shore water again, "how did you like it?"

Fins couldn't find the right words. The ocean was so big and the life under it so much of another world. He felt small and not much good, and he couldn't think of any words that were right.

So he just said, "Great, Newt! I'll never forget today!"

"I know what you mean," Newt said. "No matter how often you go ocean diving, this first time will be the one you will remember above all others. I still remember my first time in the ocean. There's power out there, and mystery, and it hits you all over the first time you face up to it."

The other club members began to come in now, and they gathered around Newt, showing their treasures from the sea. Shells of many kinds, star fish, sand dollars, seaweed, and fish. The men who had gone spear fishing brought in some beauties. Bob tossed a ten-pound ling cod at Betty's feet.

"There's our supper," he said.

"Good! I'm glad it isn't an octopus. I can take care of this one!"

They spent the rest of the day playing around in the shore water or planning the next day's fun.

Fins went with Newt to the boathouse, where Newt rented a boat to use the next morning.

When the moon was high over the ocean, they gathered around their campfire and sang songs until they were all so sleepy they were beginning to chirp instead of sing. The tents had been set up early in the afternoon, and now they all began to find their way to a sleeping place. To-morrow would be a big day.

Fins, Newt, Bob, and Hank were in the same tent. In no time at all, the camp was very quiet, except for the end-less song of the sea.

I like that coming and going of the sea, Fins thought in a sleepy way. It's big and it's little, big and little, but it goes on and on and never stops.

What a good song for sleeping!

12.

THE ABALONE HUNT

Next morning the abalone hunters went out at low tide.

Fins was all atingle to get going, but he had to wait for Bob's last check-up so he would be sure to know who was going.

"Well, here we go, just a bunch of shore pickers!" Bob said. "We'll go out from shore a little way and then dive to fifteen or twenty feet. I think we can get our limit easy out there and have a lot of fun doing it."

He told them a little about ab hunting, but most of the divers had gone before and knew a lot about it. He showed Fins how to use the iron.

"Main thing is to get your iron under his shell and pry him off. Don't give the ab a chance to clamp his shell on the rock. When you get the trick of it, you'll find you do it better with your hands. But it's best to use the iron at first.

"Another thing, don't go ab-happy, like the guy who almost got caught by the tide yesterday. If people get greedy about taking more than they should, in a few years there will be no abalone hunting for anyone."

Bob and Fins worked together. It was hard to get the first ab, and Bob had to help him finish the job. The ab was big and had a foot that clung to his rock as if it had grown there. Next time Fins tackled one a little smaller, and this one he got on his own. Bob had his limit in a short time.

Fins had to work harder with each one and go up for air more often. When he got each ab, it meant a trip up to the float. Just as he was about to take his last ab, Fins saw a very big one on a rock ahead. What a big beauty it was!

I could get it myself too! I know I could! he thought. But then I'd have six. One of them would have to go back into the sea. H'm! Just one over the limit wouldn't matter. Rules! Everywhere a guy turned he found some kind of rule!

Bob had gone up with his last ab. He seemed to give no thought at all to coming back for another one.

Guess I'd better go up, Fins thought. I need air. I can always come down again. Suddenly, Fins Harper felt ashamed of what he had been thinking. He was a SCUBA now, and he'd better not forget it!

He followed Bob to the surface, and he didn't even look back at the big abalone on the rock.

Everyone had his limit of five, for this was a good place for ab hunting. Mary had known a good place when she saw one.

"How about eats for you sea hunters now?" Betty asked.

"That's just what we need!" Bob answered happily.

Soon the air was heavy with the wonderful fragrance of fish cooking over a campfire. As they sat around eating and talking about the hunt and other skin diving fun, Fins saw something far out at sea. What could it be?

"What is that thing, Bob? Looks like a cork bobbing up and down out there."

Bob looked at the far horizon, watching the dark spot Fins had first seen.

"Looks like a boat," he said, "but it isn't the one Newt went on."

The boat, or whatever it was, seemed to be going no place at all. But it was so far out that it was hard to tell for sure.

Suddenly Bob said, "I think I know what that is. I read about the plan somewhere, and I'll just bet that's it. It's a floating lab!"

"A floating lab? What in heck is that?" Fins asked.

"Well, you see, people of science are trying to find out all they can about mineral and food supplies in the ocean, because we might need them someday. They know that there is a lot of magnesium out there in that water, but they have to find out just what level of water is the best place to find it. So colleges send these floating labs out here to make tests at the different water levels. They find new kinds of fish, too, and they try to find out whether they are good to eat. We might need to know someday."

"I guess they have some good skin divers out there," Fins remarked.

"They have the best skin divers they can get, and all the latest in suits and gear. It would be great to work with a crew like that," Bob said, in a wishful way.

"Why don't you, then?" Fins asked.

Fins knew he wouldn't be old enough yet, but someday he would. But if Bob wanted work like that, why didn't he go after it?

"Main thing is I quit school to go to work and I just didn't get back. Now it seems a little too late. Those fellows on that crew are not only the best skin divers that you'll find anywhere, but they are also top-notch men of science. They are probably all graduates of the biggest colleges in the country, or will be very soon. Well, that's that! It's a good job for a diver if he can get it, which I can't. . . ."

Bob changed the subject.

Fins tried to follow what Bob was saying about spear fishing, but he couldn't turn off his thinking about that floating lab.

There must be some kind of diving I can do without going back to school, he thought. I'll ask Bob. Maybe he knows something besides the floating lab.

"Bob, isn't there any way a top-notch skin diver can make a good living without getting all tangled up with college and stuff like that?"

Bob shrugged.

"I don't know of anything around here. The South Sea boys make a living on sponge diving, and some on pearl diving. You've heard about the brown-skinned fellows who dive for money the tourists throw overboard. But what a way to live! I don't think we could have the kind of living we are used to here on what those fellows make. I wouldn't want to do it. I pick up a little money doing small diving jobs, same as you are already doing. Once in awhile I get a call to help recover the body of someone who has drowned. That usually pays a little. . . ."

"That sounds gruesome!" Fins commented.

"Oh, not too bad, unless the body's been in the water a long time. It's always sad, though, even when it's a grown person who didn't obey the rules of water sport. The worst is a little kid that wandered off and got swept away. I've brought up two like that, and they're rough, *real* rough. The best jobs, the top-notch pay kind, are those that take more education than I'll ever have. Like those fellows out in the boat."

"Thanks, Bob, I was just curious."

Once again Fins felt his hopes go down, away down, and not in the abyss of an ocean, either. But he didn't have time to feel sorry for himself, for Bob was speaking again.

"How about a little diving pretty soon? Might get some nice shells. I'll go out with anyone who wants to go."

Fins had his answer ready on that one!

"Count me in!" he said.

This time it was much easier to get into the surf because he knew what to expect.

They tried several depths, and each place had its own strange sea life. Fins wished they could find some coral, but he knew there would be none this far north. He'd have to go to the tropics for that.

And I'll go there someday, too, he thought. I'm going to dive every place a skin diver has ever gone, and some places they haven't gone! I'll even go places where I'll be the first one there.

He looked on the sandy ledge and among the rocks for starfish. It would be fun to take a good specimen home to study. He found several, but not what he wanted. At last he saw an especially good one, and when he had it loose from the rock, Bob was giving the up sign.

Gosh! I didn't know we'd been down that long! Time goes so fast . . . or just stands still. Or you just don't care about time. I guess that's it.

Newt had been back for a few minutes, and everyone was around him, listening to the stories he and Hank told about the sea life they had found on the offshore reef.

"I can't wait to get those pictures," Newt said. "Then you'll see what I saw! . . . if they're any good."

"How about that boat out yonder?" Bob asked. "I thought it was a fishing lab. Right?"

"Right. This time they're trying to find why the crab fishermen are finding so many dead crabs in their nets and traps."

"Do they know why yet?" Fins asked.

"They think they do, but they have to do some more testing. They think the nets have been going down to a level that's short on oxygen for some reason or other. If that's it, they'll tell the fishermen to raise their nets a few feet to a level where the water has enough oxygen. That ought to do it."

As Fins listened to this, he was thrilled all over about the important things a good skin diver could do. But even as he felt thrilled, a cold little wave of sadness hit him. A job like that was not for him. But there must be SOMETHING just as important that a good skin diver could do without college and all that stuff. He'd just keep his eyes and ears open. That was all he could do now. Something would turn up in time.

"Well," Newt said, "I guess we've about had it. By the way, did anyone see our friend who almost drowned yesterday?"

No one had.

"Well, I guess he's out of the picture, then. Looks as if we had better get started back. By the time we break camp and get our abs all packed, along with our diving gear, it will be high time we headed for home."

Fins got busy and helped pack, just as the others did. With everyone working, it didn't take long to have things ready and the camp clean.

What a weekend this had been! A rescue job, a lot of good fun diving in the wonderful, moving ocean, ab hunting, eating good fresh ocean fish, playing in the water like a school of porpoises, more eating, and just plain resting and visiting. Every bit of it was fun, and more than ever Fins was glad to be a SCUBA, rules and all!

13.

A NEW JOB, GAINED AND LOST

Almost before Fins had all his gear out of Newt's car, his mother came out to see them.

"Hi!" she said. "Both of you. Am I glad to see you!"

"Why?" Fins asked. "You didn't worry about me, I hope!"

"I didn't have much time to worry," she said. "That telephone has been driving me crazy all weekend, and everybody wants you . . . never me!"

This was a big surprise to Fins, for almost no one called him, unless it was about a small diving job, and that didn't happen often. Not nearly often enough!

"Well, I must roll along," Newt said.

Then he spoke to Mrs. Harper.

"See? I brought this fellow back without a scratch. He even helped rescue someone who didn't have the good sense a diver always needs. But I'll let him tell you about that. Hope you come to our big final check-out at the pool in a couple of weeks, Mrs. Harper. You'll see Fins doing a lot of this underwater stuff, and I think you'll be proud of him. Plan to come, won't you?"

"Well, maybe," Mrs. Harper answered doubtfully. I'll think about it."

"O.K. Think hard. 'Bye, now!"

Fins watched the red car until it turned the corner. Then he said, "Now, Mom, how about those phone calls?"

"Well, two were about jobs . . ."

"Jobs? Two at once? Wow! Tell me quick!"

Fins picked up his bright new tank and started into the house. His mother carried his fins and mask.

"One was from Mr. Corliss. He thinks he has a job in a grocery store for you this fall. That would be nice, wouldn't it? You're to call him in the morning. The other job was something at the college. They want a skin diver to help them get something out in the river. Then there were a couple of calls from boys, but they wouldn't give their names."

"H'm. Might be Rich. The same boy both times?" Fins was cleaning his diving things as he talked.

"No, I don't think so. One said he might call again. The other boy just hung up when I asked for his number. Sort of a bad-tempered voice. He could do with some manners."

Fins couldn't think of anyone he knew who had a voice like that. Unless it was Hooker. But why would this character called Hooker want to talk to him? We aren't exactly buddies, he said to himself.

Aloud he said, "How about this call from the college? When do I call, or do they call me?"

His mother gave him a piece of paper with the number.

"Call this number in the morning at ten," she said.

"What a weekend!" Fins said, laughing. "First time I leave the place, everything happens. A lot happened where I was too."

"Tell me!"

His mother had never shown much interest in his diving before, so he made the most of it. But suddenly, he knew he was very sleepy. The salt sea air, the work and fun of diving, all the excitement, and the long drive home, were beginning to tell on him.

He yawned sleepily.

"Guess we'd better go to bed," his mother said. "I think you have a big week ahead."

That big week began the next morning when Fins phoned Mr. Corliss.

"We have a job for you, I think," Mr. Corliss said. "How would you like to be a carry-out boy in a grocery store?"

"Sounds O.K.," Fins answered. "Where is it?"

Mr. Corliss told him.

The store wasn't far from home, which was good.

Almost at once Fins knew he would like Mr. Andrews, the manager.

"You won't always be a carry-out boy," Mr. Andrews said. "That is, if you do a good job, and I think you will. You can get some pretty good jobs in the grocery business."

Fins liked Mr. Andrews, but one thing bothered him.

"I don't know about being a grocery-store worker all my life," he said. "I want to be a skin diver someday."

Mr. Andrews looked at Fins closely.

"A SKIN DIVER? Now, how in the world could a skin diver earn a living?"

"Oh, lots of ways, if he's real good," Fins answered.

But somehow he didn't feel like saying much more about it to Mr. Andrews. Here was a man who liked grocery stores, and all the interest he would have in diving would be because he sold canned sea food in his store!

"Well, I like your looks, boy," Mr. Andrews said. "That teacher of yours seems to think you'll do O. K., so if you want the job you can have it. You might get to liking grocery-store work so much you'd change your mind about working up in it. People do change their minds, you know."

Fins smiled, but inside himself he said, Don't count on me changing my mind, Mr. Andrews! Just don't count on it!

Fins was to begin his new job on the following Monday. That would give him a week to find a boy for his paper route. That wouldn't be hard, for there was always a long list of boys wanting paper routes.

Next, was his call to the college. That was the real thrill!

"Yes," said Professor Roberts, "we need a good skin diver. But I think I should tell you that we really need a diver who knows a lot about geology. We have no geology student who is also a good skin diver, but if one comes along, you would be out of a job. If you want to make some dives for us until a person like that shows up, we'd be glad to have you."

"Sure, I'll take it," Fins answered. "When do I start? I'll have to bring another diver with me. My club won't let me go on dives alone."

"That's all right," the professor answered. "Come over this afternoon, and we'll send you down for some rock we want."

Mel was busy, so Fins got Rich to go with him.

On the way over, Fins tried to find out where Rich had gone with Hooker. But Rich shut up like one of the clams Fins had seen at the ocean. Rich was friendly, but he just wasn't talking. So Fins dropped the subject of Hooker.

During the next week Fins made four diving trips for the college. The professors and students were friendly, and they knew a lot of interesting things about the sea and mountains. Fins listened as hard as he could, though sometimes they used words much too hard for him. Now and then he found himself wishing he could understand their strange language better, but he didn't spend too much time thinking about it. His days were full of other interesting things to do.

Then one day, at the end of his fourth trip for the college, the blow fell.

"You've done good work for us, Fins," Professor Roberts said, "but you know I said we really wanted a student who is also a good skin diver. Today that student came into the office, so we won't need you any more."

Fins felt his heart going down, down. Of course, Professor Roberts DID say that, but somehow Fins didn't believe it would happen. Not this soon, anyway.

"I can come and help sometimes, can't I?" he asked.

"I wish I could say 'yes,' " the professor said, "but you see, you have to go down and knock off rock and other things and bring them up to us. You bring up samples of silt and water plants, but we don't get to see these things just the way they were seen by you. Now, if you knew a lot about earth and water science you could go down and make a report on what you found. We would know just what it was like, and nothing would be disturbed down there. That is why we need a geology student for this job. Or, if we need samples, you could bring up just what we need and no more. Maybe someday you'll know all these things, too, and with your skill as a skin diver, you'll be a top-notch marine scientist. Thank you so much for helping us. You'll get a check from the college very soon."

"Thank you, Professor Roberts. I see how it is."

And he did understand, but he didn't like it.

Once more his hands were tied to keep him from doing a really important diving job, all because he didn't know a lot of other things.

But I'm not giving up, he thought fiercely. There must

be SOMETHING a skin diver can do to make a good living without doing a lot of hard old book studying first!

When the check came a few days later, Fins put it with other money he was saving for a neoprene suit of his own. He was glad for the check, but he felt a letdown, too, for it reminded him once more of a job he had liked a lot, but couldn't keep.

His work as carry-out boy at the grocery store went along well enough, but more than ever he knew he didn't want to be in a grocery store all his life. He lived from one weekend to another, for it was on the weekends that he went out with the SCUBA club.

Although he was busy he kept up with the class at the Y. He thought he knew a lot about skin diving, but every class time gave him something new to learn and to think about.

The high point of the class was the last session, for that was the time when the divers would show how much they had learned. There would be fun contests, and some serious things, but all of it would be the kind of thing a bunch of skin divers would enjoy.

His mother promised she would go. That was a happy turn of events, although Fins was not as surprised as he would have been a couple of months ago. She no longer made a big fuss every time he wanted to go out with the club.

When the night came for the last class, Margaret Harper was there watching, with others, the fun in the pool.

Newt called the divers together. "Tonight you're going through all the things you've learned in this class, but you're going to do it for speed. First, we'll take buddy breathing."

Once more Fins found himself counted off with Mary. She was pretty good now, but still a little small to handle her tank easily. They came in third on the buddy breathing.

They had to run a race taking a tank to a diver under water, get the old one off and the new one on. Fins tied for second on that.

But the races he did best were those where he could be on his own. The marble one, especially.

"Do you have all your marbles?" Newt called.

Everyone laughed.

"Well, if you don't have, you're going to get a chance to get all your marbles. We'll play that everyone needs seven marbles to get along in the world. You will go out in fours, find seven marbles on the bottom of the pool, and come back. You must remove your mask under water and put it back, and you can only go after one marble at a time."

Fins found himself with Rich, Bob, and Hank.

And he won the contest! When he brought his seventh marble up and gave it to Newt he couldn't help but look over at his mother. She was laughing and clapping as hard as anybody.

As Fins put that seventh marble down with the other six, he felt he had done more than win a diving contest with a bunch of marbles. Now his mother would be with him in his skin-diving fun. No more fights at home over it!

After the fun was over, everyone crowded around the winners, laughing and slapping each other's wet backs.

"Well, Mrs. Harper," Newt said, "you've seen for yourself how good these swimmers have to be to stay in a skin-diving club."

"Yes, I see," she admitted. "Swimming does look like fun. I still don't go for that diving stuff, but it *is* exciting, and Fins seems to do pretty well. I guess I might as well give in to the idea that he will be a diver."

"Fins is a swell diver," Newt said with emphasis, "but he should take that lifesaving class. When he's finished that, he'll be able to take care of himself in any water that's safe for humans to be in at all."

"Oh yes, he must take that!" Fins's mother agreed. "If he's going to be waterlogged all his life, he might as well learn all the tricks of it!"

Although that night was the end of one class group at the Y, the next week began another. This second class was even more fun.

Fins worked with the lifesaving teacher, and he enjoyed every minute of it. He learned to make a drowning person cooperate with the rescuer. He learned what to do if they were too scared to cooperate. Slap them, that's what!

"And if he fights you, knock him out!" the teacher said.

"Sounds rough, but a drowning person does sometimes fight. He's so scared he doesn't know what he's doing. You may have to choose between knocking him out and letting him drown."

Fins learned how to make a drowning victim start breathing again. It was all interesting and fun, for he felt himself learning.

But the summer wasn't all just one big dive after another. There was his job at the grocery store that took a lot of time. Best of all was the nice fat check he got every Saturday night. He always gave his mother a big slice of it to help on home bills, but even then he had more money left for himself than he had ever had. Each payday brought him that much nearer his goal—the best underwater outfit any lung diver could get!

One day Mr. Corliss came into the store to see him.

"Hi, Fins!" he greeted. "How's it going here?"

"Just fine, Mr. Corliss!" Fins answered. "Thanks a million for getting me this job. I'm saving my money and by next spring I'll have enough to get everything a good skin diver needs . . . the best of everything too!"

Mr. Corliss laughed.

"Well, I see you're still water-happy!"

"You bet I am! Someday I'll find a good skin-diving job I can do, and then I'll have it made."

"I hope it works out for you, Fins," Mr. Corliss answered. "But look, if you change your mind about coming back to school, you can, you know. Tomorrow is registration day, and you can come back if you want to. You haven't been kicked out by any means. Mr. Andrews knows all about it, and he'd let you quit without holding it against you. He'd even let you work after school and on Saturdays."

This time Fins didn't get angry with Mr. Corliss for talking about school. He knew Mr. Corliss was only interested in him, and all a teacher could ever see was school. You couldn't blame him for that. Just the way a teacher is put together! But it's not for me, he thought.

"Thanks, Mr. Corliss. It's good to know that, but I just want to be a skin diver, a top-notch one. I don't want to go back to school. If I could study ocean science and all that without that other junk, I'd come back, I think. But I can't. I may be sorry someday, but I don't think so. Anyway, that's the way it is now."

"O.K., Fins," Mr. Corliss answered. "We won't argue any more about it. There's something I hope you'll do, though. If you don't do it for your own good, do it for me."

"What's that, Mr. Corliss?" Fins asked. He would do a lot for Mr. Corliss.

"Get yourself a card at the city library and check out books on marine science. They have a pretty good list there, and you can learn a lot on your own. Then if you get a chance someday to take an examination for a job where knowing marine science would help, you'll have a lot of it stored up in your head."

Fins thought a minute. Well, that sounded like good sense. After the diving season was over, he'd have time to do things like that. Books about the ocean ought to be pretty good reading too.

"O.K., Mr. Corliss," he said, "I'll try that. Can't hurt me, I guess."

That very night after work Fins went to the library. He was surprised to find so many books about the sea and ocean life. Some of them looked like hard reading. He'd leave those alone. But some looked as if they'd be fun. So he took out a card and brought home his first load of books on ocean science.

The next day his friends went by the store in big and little groups, and by ones and twos, laughing, talking, teasing each other. It was registration day at the high school, and this time Fins didn't have to go.

He was glad he didn't have to go, and yet there was a strange feeling deep inside when he saw these closed little groups forming. He had never been on the outside looking in, before.

But then, on second thought, he had SCUBA. He was surely on the inside of that ... very deep inside. And that was what he wanted. You can't be on the inside of every gang of fellows. And who wants to be, anyway?

Fins picked up a big bag of groceries and followed a customer to her car. He didn't hear what the lady was saying, though he had the feeling she was talking.

He couldn't keep his eyes from wandering here and there, following, as long as he could see them, the groups of noisy kids going up the hill to Del Rio High School.

14.

A MYSTERIOUS DIVING JOB

As THE weeks went on, Fins missed Mel and his other school friends more than he had ever thought he would. If he heard a young voice somewhere around the store, he'd look up quickly, wondering which of his school buddies it might be. But it was seldom any of them.

After one of these disappointments, he scolded himself for even thinking about them.

They're in school, idiot! You won't be seeing those guys around much, but that's O.K. You want it this way; they want it that way. What are you kicking about? Not a thing, not a blamed thing!

Oh well, once in awhile some of them come in after school. That's enough to keep in touch, isn't it? He'd hurry with his work so he wouldn't be too pushed if some of them should come in around four o'clock!

Four o'clock! Paper-route time! Now, why did he even think of that? He didn't have to bother with a paper route any more. He had a steady job, an eight-hour-a-day job. He was helping his mother keep up their home. And what did he need of those guys who went to school, anyway?

Maybe he didn't need them, but he kept looking for them. At first he did, anyway. Sometimes they did come in, alone, or in small groups, talking about things that were no longer a part of his life.

And they were always in a hurry! Always just coming from someplace or going someplace, or headed home after being someplace.

"Hi, Dick!" he'd call, maybe to Dick Carter, whom he used to know quite well. "Where you goin' in such a hurry? Got fire on your feet?"

Dick had turned, looked surprised, then said, "Oh, Fins, it's you! How you doin', old boy? Well, it's good to see you. Gotta go now. I'm goin' out for football practice."

And so it went. They'd ask how he was doing, but they didn't really care. They had their own world, the school world. He used to be a part of it, but he wasn't now. So what? Who cared, anyway?

One afternoon a gang of laughing kids came in, goofing off all over the place, loading up with a good supply of snacks for the trip on the rooters' bus.

As Fins bagged their candy bars, potato chips, peanuts, gum, and such, he couldn't help chanting an old yell with them:

We're gonna win-win!
We're gonna win-win!
WOW!
We're gonna win-win!

We're gonna win-win
    HOW?
    EASY!
That's how, Del Rio High!

Suddenly they were all gone and the store was deadly quiet. A hard knot seemed to form in Fins's stomach. He couldn't name it, but it was definitely there. It made him uneasy and uncomfortable. He wished something would happen to take his mind off that crazy, happy gang.

And something did happen.

Rich Morton came into the store. That alone was unusual, for this store wasn't in Rich's neighborhood.

He came to see Fins, which was even more unusual. It was the first time Rich had sought Fins out for anything. Right now, Fins would have gone off with the Pied Piper himself. He felt so lonely and left out of things. But it wasn't the Pied Piper, playing an enticing tune to make him follow. It was only Rich Morton, with a big scheme in his head.

"Wanta make some extra money?" Rich asked.

"Sure. Who doesn't?" Fins countered.

"An easy diving job for a guy I know," Rich explained. "Won't need tanks. I could do it myself, but he wants it done this evening and two can work faster than one, as you know. Thought you might like to get in on it. I'm getting twenty-five bucks and I'll split with you."

Jeepers! Twelve and a half for a couple of hours' work at the most. It couldn't last much longer, for the sun would be down in about three hours. Mr. Andrews would probably let him off early. This had been a light day. But he did want to know more about it. After all, he didn't know Rich very well.

"What are you supposed to be diving for?" he asked.

"A waterproof bag that weighs fifteen or twenty pounds."

"What's in it?" Fins asked curiously.

A dangerous flash came into Rich's eyes.

"Look, bud, I asked you to help me. I didn't ask for a guy with a lot of questions. When I get a diving job that pays, I take it, and I don't ask questions. I figure it's none of my business what's in the bag. They're payin' me to bring it up. I get the bag, they pay me, and that's all I care about. It had better be all you care about, too, or we won't be workin' together."

Fins didn't like Rich's answer, but after all, Rich was right that it was really none of their business what was in the bag. A postman delivered mail. He didn't ask what kind of news the letters carried.

"O.K., I grant you're right on that. But who's hiring you . . . and me, if I help you?"

"A guy named Tripe Martin. Does that mean anything to you?"

"Not a thing."

"Didn't think it would. He's hiring me, and I'm hiring you. O.K.? Any more questions?"

Rich's voice cut Fins down to the size of a five-year-old, but he swallowed his irritation. After all, twelve and a half bucks was quite a step toward his new neoprene suit. And this might lead to other jobs with Rich, for somehow Rich got next to paying jobs that nobody else seemed to know about.

"I'll go," Fins answered.

They made final arrangements; Mr. Andrews gave him time off, and Fins left with Rich.

Mrs. Harper wasn't home from work yet. Fins scribbled a note for his mother, got his diving gear, and went off with Rich.

The late sun of a September afternoon put bronze glints on the lazy river. As always, the very sight of a river made Fins glad to be alive, glad to be able to dive. He could hardly wait to get his gear on and become part of that river.

This was a little-used part of the river. The brush was thick right down to the water's edge. It was a hard part to find, and a harder one to reach.

"Sort of an odd place to lose a waterproof bag," Fins commented.

"Like I said, I ask no questions," Rich retorted.

They made several attempts to find the bag along the shore, with no success. On a trip up for air, Fins said, "Doesn't this guy have any idea where he left ... I mean, lost, that bag?" Fins asked.

"Not too much," Rich answered. "This is the general spot he told me about. He was in a hurry, I guess, and didn't take time to mark the place."

In a hurry? That much of a hurry, that he couldn't take

time to mark the location of a bag he was willing to pay twenty-five dollars to have again? But this time Fins kept his curiosity inside himself. Instead, he suggested a circle search.

"I think a circle search is about the only chance we have to find it before sunset."

"O.K.," Rich agreed. "We don't have very good equipment for it, but I guess we can make do. I have a coil of light rope in the car."

Rich got the rope, and they fastened one end to an almost submerged willow near the shore. Then Rich pulled the slack out to the end and began his search. Fins kept on paddling around near the shore, reasoning that a fellow in a hurry to drop something wouldn't have time to get far from shore. But then, the current was pretty strong here, and if the bag happened to hit a fairly clear bottom section, it might be eased out toward midstream.

That was just what had happened! In a few moments Rich called, "Here it is! Wedged between a couple of big rocks. Come and help me get it out!"

Fins swam out to Rich, and in a few moments they had the bag free from its rocky prison. It was indeed heavy for the size of it. What was in it? Fins wanted to make some guesses, but Rich's attitude about curious people being what it was, he kept still.

They had almost reached the bank when Fins's arm, in the arc of a stroke, hit something that felt very odd. He swam to it. He couldn't see well, but well enough to know that the object lay in the general shape of a human body.

He reached a hand to it. What in the world was it? An old fallen tree with rags dumped on it and slime gathered?

A strange, mushy softness met his touch. He lifted a branchlike part of the object.

What he saw sent him to the surface . . . up for air, and for Rich!

"Hey, Rich! I—I found a—a—body! A man's body!"

Rich had reached the bank now. He tossed his rope and the waterproof bag up to a safe point and swam back to Fins.

"Gosh! You're right!" he said. "And the old boy's been here a long time! Some poor tramp that nobody missed, I guess. Look what's left of his clothes!"

"Rich! We've got to report this!" Fins exclaimed.

"Report it? I don't know why! You just better not! There's been nothing in the papers about a murder, or anybody missing, not for a long time. If we report it, there's gonna be a lot of questioning."

"So what?" Fins asked. "We weren't doing anything so awful. We can prove when we came, and why. Nothing's gonna happen to us, but it sure will if later it comes out that we did know something about this guy!"

"Nobody's gonna know a thing, if you've got the sense you were born with!" Rich was almost shouting now, he was so angry.

"Rich, I don't care what you do, but I'm gonna report

this! I found this body, and I'm gonna say so!" Fins's voice was heavy with determination.

"Then you'd better keep me out of it! If you don't, I have friends who can take care of you!" Rich threatened. "And you can forget your dough for this job!"

"That's O.K.!" Fins answered angrily. "Something tells me I made the big mistake of my life to come out here with you!"

"And I made a bigger one to ask you!" Rich retorted.

Silently they dressed and loaded their gear into Rich's car. The ride back was just as silent. When Rich let Fins off at his home, Rich's only comment was, "Now, remember, you keep my name off that rolling tongue of yours!"

"I can do that!" Fins answered.

When Fins told his mother she was, of course, upset about the whole thing.

"What you do get into!" she said. "But there's nothing to do but report the finding of the body. You'd better call that diving teacher. He'll know whom you should call."

Fins dialed Newt's number. Briefly, he told him the story, leaving out Rich's name, as he had promised.

"I'll be right over, and bring Captain Barber with me," Newt answered.

He was as good as his word. Captain Barber and Newt both tried their best to get Fins to give the name of his companion, but Fins refused every line of argument.

"You were either alone or you weren't!" Newt said, gruffly, for him. "If you had a companion, an officer of the law is entitled to all the information a citizen can give. If you were alone, then you broke a very important SCUBA rule. You know the penalty for a first offense of that kind!"

"Yes," Fins answered, "a two weeks' suspension from club activities."

"Well," said Captain Barber, "I guess that's it. You're to stay in town, available, young man. Tomorrow I'll get a couple of divers the coroner usually hires for jobs like this. We can't do anything for the poor fellow in the river now, and probably we couldn't even find the body, dark as it is." He turned to Fins's mother. "Thank you, Mrs. Harper, for your cooperation. If this young man changes his mind and decides to give the name of his buddy, just give me a call. It's a pretty fine line to draw between what the kids call 'squealing' and what the law calls withholding information. We don't want to keep Fins in custody. As far as I can see, he hasn't done anything wrong. I do think he's using poor judgment right now, for it looks as if his buddy may have his reasons for keeping under cover . . . something not at all connected with finding this body. Mr. Browning here will take care of one angle of this thing, and that will be enough for the time being."

"Thank you, sir," Margaret Harper replied.

There was no use discussing this further. She knew Fins wouldn't change his mind. He'd take his punishment and keep his mouth shut. She could only hope there were no other serious complications in the case.

Fins followed the men to the door, walking as if he had weight shoes on both feet. This time he was really low man with Newt Browning, and that hurt. Yet he felt that Newt understood why he couldn't squeal. But Newt had a job to do too. Each was doing what he felt he had to do, and that was that.

A brief news item a few days later told of the finding of a partially decomposed body in the American River, identified as John Slocum, one of the city's derelicts, missing for a month or more. Autopsy showed a heart attack, with the body probably rolling down the bank and into the river. The paper stated that the body had been found by a fifteen-year-old skin diver. No name was given. That book was closed.

But it wasn't closed for Fins Harper. The two weeks of his suspension went very slowly. His friends in the club sympathized with him, but they also knew that Newt couldn't do anything else but suspend Fins. Club members themselves had made that rule and had fixed the penalty for breaking it. The regulation against going skin diving alone was absolute.

One thing Fins had learned was that he had gone out on a job with Rich Morton for the last time. Never again would he knowingly team up with him for anything.

Rich came into the store one day and offered a vague apology.

"Gosh, Fins! I didn't think about this happening to you. I'm the one that oughta be suspended. I'm sure sorry!"

"Come clean, then!" Fins retorted. "That's all it would take."

"It's not that simple!" Rich answered shortly.

Fins had no more to say to Rich Morton. He went back to the stock room to unpack boxes. In a few minutes he heard Rich's car clatter down the street.

His time of suspension was nearly over. The two weeks had seemed like two months. He couldn't go diving with SCUBA members, and he seldom saw Mel.

He and Mel were still good friends, and they went diving together now and then . . . if Mel didn't have anything else to do. But more and more Mel did have something else to do.

It was after one of these dives together that they got back late. Fins was to help on the evening shift and he almost didn't get to work on time.

Fins had his complete outfit now, including the best neoprene suit that money could buy. He just had to show it off to Mel, who was properly impressed. It had been such fun, swimming and diving around with Mel, enjoying his new equipment, that he didn't notice how fast and deep the shadows had come.

Mel lived quite near the store, so he said, "Leave your stuff here. It will be O.K. You can pick up your things tomorrow, or any time.

"That was a cold dive today, and I don't think I want to go any more this fall. You have a neoprene suit, and for you that's good. But diving just doesn't mean that much to me. You can leave your things here any time; then you can go right from work."

"Thanks, Mel. Guess I'll do that. What if no one is home when I want to get my gear?"

"Oh, I think someone will be around. But if they aren't, you know the secret way to my room."

"O.K., thanks."

This was October, and, like Mel said, he wouldn't be diving much until warm weather. Of course, he'd go to the Y and dive sometimes just for fun.

Fins smiled as he remembered the secret way to Mel's room. He and Mel had worked it out in their "cops and robbers" days. They had done everything they could to make the secret way hard to find and hard to use.

What fun it had been to be with a bunch of kids and suddenly be able to drop out of sight as if the earth had swallowed them!

They would hear the kids yelling and hunting, with no luck at all. Then when the kids had been about to give up, he and Mel would open the front door and call.

"Hey, you guys! Pipe down! We're right here. What's all the fuss?"

The look on those kids' faces was really something!

Of course, he remembered the secret way to Mel's room. He even remembered exactly the way the key hung on a rusty old spike high on a tree trunk by his window.

It was all kid stuff; he knew that now. But what was wrong with remembering kid stuff, especially when the remembering was such fun?

He probably wouldn't be using the secret way again, but it was fun to think about it. There was no hurry about getting his diving gear. Maybe next week he'd get it and go to the Y after work. His suspension was over now. It would be good to be with the SCUBA gang again. Like Mel said, it was too cold to dive anyplace outside the pool, unless you had the right kind of suit.

It was Saturday night, and cleanup took a long time. Fins swept out the store while Mr. Andrews counted the money and put it into his safe.

About ten o'clock, Mr. Andrews said, "Well, that about ties it up, Frank. You go on home now. I'll finish and lock up."

"Sure I'm done, Mr. Andrews? If there's anything more to do, I'll be glad to do it."

"Thanks, Frank, but we're about set. Got your bike here?"

"Yes, it's right back of the store. O.K., Mr. Andrews, I'll go on, then. So long."

As Fins went through the store toward the alley where he always kept his bike, he thought again of Mel. Saturday night had always been such a good fun night. Maybe he'd stop in tonight and see Mel and hash things over a bit. He hadn't talked to him since that last dive, except to say "hi!"

On second thought he knew it would be no use. Mel had gone with the football team to an out-of-town game. Probably his whole family would be gone.

As he stepped out the back door to get his bike, someone called, "Fins!" Oh, he *thought* someone said his name.

It was such a hushed voice that he couldn't be sure. Besides, the noise of the door closing behind him, with Mr. Andrews locking it from the inside, covered the outside sound.

The voice came again . . . and it *was* a voice calling his name. This time he was sure.

"Fins! I gotta see you!" It was Rich Morton!

Fins followed the voice.

Rich stood in the shadow of a big power-line pole.

"Fins, I got a diving job for you. Fifty bucks in it!"

Fins was so completely astonished he couldn't speak for a moment. How could Rich even dare think of such a thing?

"You think I'd take another job with *you* . . . after what happened? My head isn't on backwards yet!"

"Not even for fifty bucks?" Rich's voice was almost begging.

"I didn't get a cent the other time, so your money makes no difference, how much or how little!"

"Would having it before we go make a difference?"

"Might if the job is on the level . . . which I doubt!" Fins answered.

Fins mounted his bike, anxious to be off and gone. Something about the deep shadows of the alley made him nervous.

"So long, Rich! You'll find another sucker!"

Before he could put his bike in motion, the shadows became living forms, three, counting Rich.

At that very moment a car turned the alley corner, and its light flashed on the boys' faces.

Hooker and Shot Put!

Fins gasped. He didn't like the looks of this . . . not any part of it.

Apparently Hooker felt the same about him, for he said, "What the heck did you get this guy for? That last trouble you had oughta been enough!"

"You said you wanted the fastest, best diver I knew, and Fins Harper is that one. Besides, he knows that part of the river better than I do. Even if we did have trouble before, I thought I could talk him into this job, with real money to wave under his nose." Now Rich looked almost desperate with fright and worry.

"That's right. He does know that part of the river," Hooker agreed.

At last Fins found his voice.

"Well, I don't want the job, not for any price! I'm going home!"

Hooker stepped in front of the bike.

"Oh no, you're not goin' home! And you've got a diving job, with or without pay. We've wasted too much time already. The stuff we want brought up has to be out of town tonight. Get off that bike and come along!"

Fins pulled his fist back for a swift thrust to Hooker's chin, but he never made contact. Hooker grabbed him, and Shot Put shoved a gun into his ribs. Fins glanced at the gun, then just beyond them to their souped-up car, which was running.

"Hey, you guys!" Rich said angrily. "You said there wouldn't be any gun stuff in this!"

"Shut up!" Shot Put growled in a low, threatening voice. "Get going, both of you! Get in that car, and fast. And you, Morton, since you're so interested in guns, look!"

Hooker pulled a stubby, but very deadly gun from his pocket and carelessly shoved it under Rich's nose.

"Cute, ain't it? Get goin'!"

"Fins, I didn't know it would be like this. Honest, I didn't! These guys know a lot of little, shady stuff I've been into. Nothin' too bad, but they add up to trouble. They've been making all kinds of threats and . . ."

"They ain't just threats, buddy. We'd carry out any one of 'em and go home laughin'! Don't you forget it!"

They reached the car, and Hooker ordered them both into the back. He drove, while Shot Put kept his gun on the boys.

"What are we supposed to be diving for? Gold?" Fins asked.

Shot Put laughed harshly.

"Gold!" he exclaimed. "One little ol' ounce of this stuff brings a lot more than a whole pound of gold. We wouldn't fool with gold. That's peanuts!"

Hooker began talking to Shot Put just then, and they paid no more attention to their passengers, except to keep a watchful eye on them and the gun on them.

"What in heck are they talking about?" Fins asked Rich in a low voice.

"Dope," Rich answered quietly. "A dope peddler in

town has a batch of the stuff from Shanghai. He got tailed and had to get rid of it. Same thing as we brought up three weeks ago. Hooker and Shot Put are his go-betweens. They took this new batch and tossed it into the river. It's in a waterproof bag, same as the other. Now this big guy wants his stuff. He thinks he has a good chance to get out of town with it tonight. He'll come back when things cool down. But if he waits now, he'll probably get caught, beside losing that bag of stuff in the river. Hooker and Shot Put can't dive, but I can. I've done quite a lot of diving for them. They pay good and I asked no questions . . . like I told you before. Lots of times I wished I hadn't got mixed up in it, but the money looked good, and I didn't know until that job three weeks ago that I was diving for dope. Honest, I didn't! I came to get you tonight because I couldn't think of any other diver good enough to do what these guys want. Besides, I was getting scared plenty!"

Fins didn't answer. He didn't even look at Rich's worried face. He was thinking—harder than he'd ever thought in his life. If he could only get word to Newt, tell him to get the cops . . . if only . . .

He leaned forward and spoke to Hooker.

"My diving stuff is at Mel Hanson's," he said, "and I'll have to call Mom so she won't worry. She might even get the cops after *me* if I don't show up pretty close to when I'm supposed to."

"O.K., mamma's baby," Hooker sneered. "Call her, but

I'm gonna be right there listenin', so be careful what you say. Mighty careful!"

Just ahead was an outside telephone booth. Hooker pulled up by it and stopped.

"How about my bike?" Fins asked. "We gotta go back after my bike! Somebody might steal it!"

"So what?" Shot Put asked. "Anyway, they probably won't. Guess you didn't see how flat those two bike tires were!"

"You think of everything!" Fins said angrily.

"Well, get out and get that phone call over with!" Hooker ordered.

Fins called his mother, while Hooker stood at the door of the booth, listening, and Shot Put kept the gun on Rich, who was still in the car.

"Look, Mom, I'm going over to Newt's for awhile. He has some new books on diving. He said I could borrow them. O.K.?"

"It's pretty late already, Fins. Don't be out too much longer," she said.

"I won't," he promised, "but it's Saturday night, you know."

"Oh, that's right. Well, O.K. I'll call Newt if you don't get in by morning!"

"You do that!" Fins said, with a laugh.

If I know my mother, she'll call him long before that, he thought. And that's O.K. too. This is once I'm glad she's that kind of a worry wart!

"Rich says you have a new tank," Hooker said. "Come on, let's get goin'!"

"My tank isn't at home," Fins said. "I left it at Mel's when we came back from a dive yesterday."

"All the better," Hooker answered. "Then your Mom won't wonder why her baby boy came home to get his little ol' swimmin' tank this time of night!"

Hooker laughed loudly at his own joke, or what he thought was a joke.

"Shut up!" ordered Shot Put. "That wasn't so funny!"

Fins felt himself getting angry all over. What if he pulled his fist and let ol' Hooker have it? Right in the mug?

Just then, Shot Put, as if reading his thought, gave the gun an extra push into his ribs.

So Fins Harper didn't give anyone a push in the mug.

"Where is Mel's place?" Hooker asked. "Now, give us the straight on it. Both these guns are loaded!"

"Mel and his folks went to a football game. Their house will be locked."

Fins was glad now that Mel was gone. Maybe these guys would decide he couldn't help, after all.

But he wasn't to be let off so easily.

"Should have rented a tank when we got the other stuff," Shot Put said.

"Well, we didn't. Counted on this guy having his own."

Then to Fins, Hooker said, "Don't you know how to get into Mel's place? You've been there enough, I'll bet."

"They lock up tight and take the keys," Fins said.

"Well, we can always break in," Hooker answered. "Don't like to on a job like this, but we will if we have to."

Suddenly Fins thought of something . . . the secret way to Mel's room . . . and the rusty hook!

"I know a way to get in," he said. "I'll go in and put the tank and things out the window."

"O.K. I'll go in with you just to make sure you don't get any ideas about using the phone," Shot Put said.

When they got to the Hanson home, Hooker stopped in the alley back of the house.

"Now, get goin'," Hooker ordered. "Get that tank out here . . . on the double! Rich and I will stay and keep my gun company until you call from a window. Then we'll come and get the tank. But hurry! It's late, and those people may come back!"

If only they would! Fins thought. I'd give anything if somebody would catch us here. But I'll do what I plan, anyway.

He moved an empty oil barrel in the garage. There, under it, was the secret hole, just as he remembered it, with the short ladder leading into a tunnel. It was so dark he could feel the darkness like something wrapped around him. But he wasn't scared. He knew every inch of that tunnel. But he couldn't go fast in it. That was O.K. This time he didn't want to go fast. He went down into the tunnel, Shot Put so close behind him he could feel the guy's breath. But when they had to get down and crawl, Shot Put had trouble. He was a little on the fat side and not meant to crawl through a narrow tunnel.

Fins got quite far ahead of Shot Put, and that gave him his chance. Here was the ladder leading out of the tunnel. The key to Mel's room would be on that rusty hook high on the tree.

Fins knew what he had to do and he did it.

He gritted his teeth and punched the sharp hook into the soft part of his hand.

Wow! That hurt, but he had to do it!

"I have the key," he called back to the puffing Shot Put, "but I tore my hand on that hook. Ladder slipped when I reached for the key. I gotta get some stuff out of the bathroom and fix it up!"

"Let it go!" Shot Put yelled.

"In salt water, I would. But I heard Rich say something about the river. I don't go in the river with a cut like this!"

"You would with a gun shovin' you in," Shot Put said.

Fins was silent a moment. Shot Put was right, of course. Suddenly something else came to his mind.

"I guess you're right," he admitted, "but then, there's the little matter of getting my blood on your car. I bleed a lot when I get cut!"

"O.K.," Shot Put growled, "fix it up. But hurry, you snail!"

Fins acted as if he hurried. Shot Put mustn't know how much he was stalling for time.

What part of the river would they be going to? A part that he knew well? He knew a lot about that river. Like a flash it came to him. Sure, that was it! The old mine! The place Hooker and Shot Put wanted him and Mel to leave, and they wouldn't. Hooker knew that Fins would know that part of the river almost as well as he knew his own house.

He grabbed the tank and his other gear and went to a window. He opened the window and called, "Here's my stuff! Good thing I've got a neoprene suit. I couldn't stay down long without one this time of year. Fact is, it's crazy to dive at all now unless it's a case of life or death!"

"Well, this is just about that!" Hooker said. "Bring that neoprene suit too. We rented one for Rich. Hurry up! Ease your tank down to me, toss the other stuff out. Then climb out the window. That'll be faster."

Fins followed directions as slowly as he could without arousing Hooker's suspicions too much. His can of powder for his neoprene suit rolled under the bed. Better leave it there. Hooker's irritation might explode. Anyway, they would surely have some with the rented suit. Then, too, he needed all the time he could get for fixing his hand.

When his gear had all been put through the window he said, "Now I gotta get some stuff for this cut."

"What cut?"

Fins told him about the spike.

Hooker turned his flashlight on Fins's hand. It was bleeding like mad.

"What a stupid thing to do! Didn't you know that spike was there?"

"I didn't remember that it stuck out so far," Fins answered.

"Well, I don't want blood all over the car, so go take

care of it, but don't try any funny stuff. I've already cut the telephone wire so don't bother to try that. Get a move on!"

Shot Put came out of the garage just then.

"You were told to follow Fins into that house! What are you doing here?"

"That tunnel ain't my size!" Shot Put wheezed. He wiped his face and wheezed again.

Hooker laughed his loud, unpleasant laugh.

"Poor Fatso! Here, you put this stuff in the car and keep an eye on Rich. I'll watch Fins!"

Hooker started through the tunnel but he came back. He had a better idea. He went to the window and called softly, "Hurry up, Fins! I give you three minutes. If you're not out here then I'll shoot!"

"I'll be out," Fins answered.

He had used his finger to write an iodine message on the wall. If only Hooker doesn't come in now! Well, he can't, unless I let him in, or he breaks in. Don't think he'll do that. Rich and I could trap these guys right now, but I'm not sure of Rich. If he helps them, I'd be a dead duck, and I mean dead! Guess I'd better play it cool.

Now, if Mel only sees that message! Don't see how he can help it. Next thing is for him to know what it means.

The message:

> Old Mine—cops
> Newt—ED 1-7181

Then he had drawn a funny, scrawly figure going into a dive. I hope he knows I'm diving, and I need him, and the cops, and Newt fast!

Fins took the iodine and some bandage with him. He knew Mel's mother wouldn't care when she knew the whole story.

Fins opened one of the big windows and dropped to the ground. He showed Hooker his crudely bandaged hand with the iodine stains seeping through.

"O.K.," said Hooker. "Now just don't pull any more stunts like that. Come on, we're off!"

What a drive that was! Fins was sure the rickety, souped-up car wouldn't hold together, but it did.

At last they came to the river where he and Mel had found the old mine. Hooker told them what to look for and about where to look.

Fins had trouble with his neoprene suit.

"Where's the powder?" he asked. "These things are hard to get on without powder."

Hooker and Shot Put looked at each other accusingly. They had forgotten to ask for powder, and apparently the man in the sports store had supposed they had some.

"How come you don't have any powder, you with a new suit like this?" Hooker demanded.

"I do, but the can rolled under Mel's bed and you were pushin' me so fast I didn't go after it. If you weren't so stupid yourself, you would have made sure you had some for your rented suit, anyway."

"Shut up!" Shot Put ordered.

At last the boys were ready to go down. They made a last check of their gear, tied one end of a rope to a tree, took the other end, and were gone . . . down, down, into the black waters.

They couldn't see a thing. A river at night had its own special darkness. All they did had to be done by feel. Their tanks held enough air for an hour, plus the reserve supply. If they came to the surface a few times, they could use air and stall for time too.

If only the Hansons would come home soon! If they didn't, that strange message on their bathroom wall wouldn't do anybody much good.

In the back of his mind was just one thought: Please come home, Mel! Please!

15.

A NOISE IN THE BRUSH

THE third time they came up, Hooker said, "I don't think you guys are even trying! That stuff is in a big waterproof bag. It's fastened to a weight like a boat anchor. Guys that can swim and dive like you can ought to find it in a few minutes. Now you try just a lot harder, or I might get nervous with this gun!"

Fins was thinking very hard and wishing he could talk to Rich. But he couldn't. He just had to think hard and hope that Rich would go along with him.

Those guys have no idea what it's like to dive after dark, he thought. Inky black, that's what ... If we can find it, and then stall for more time, when our air is about gone and we can't stall any more, we'll bring it up.

Sure enough ... when they really tried to find it, they did. Just as Hooker had said they would.

Rich thought Fins wanted to bring the bag up, but Fins put his foot on the bag. That bag must not go up yet! What if Rich didn't get the message? What if he didn't want to stall for time that way?

Suddenly, Fins knew that Rich was with him! For Rich

also put a foot on the bag and then he leaned against a rock as if he waited for something. Good old Rich! You don't belong with those guys, Fins thought. Why don't you shake 'em off?

But he couldn't ask Rich any of those things now. He couldn't even use sign language, because water visibility was zero. All he could do was wait . . . wait until the last possible moment of safety.

If only Mel would come now . . . along the bike path they always took. For if they came very close in their car, Hooker and Shot Put would see the lights. Cars almost never came down this way, so they would know something was up. Hooker might get really nervous with his gun.

Now the air was coming through very slowly, and Fins knew he must use the reserve supply. He tugged at the rope between him and Rich. Rich tugged back. They picked up the bag, with the anchor tied to it, and slowly went to the surface.

They came up a little below Hooker and Shot Put.

"How about making a run for it?" Rich whispered.

"Don't think we can make it," Fins answered. "Remember the two guns? And those guys look trigger-happy tonight."

They followed the rope to the tree, dragging the bag between them.

"Play it slow, Rich. We're in no hurry . . . see?"

"Right!" Rich answered. He purposely let himself slip on the shore rocks. He went into the water, taking the bag with him.

Fins made a great play as if helping him pull the bag out and up the bank again. He knew they couldn't do this again, but once would be accepted, and every few minutes helped.

Just as they were ready to climb up the steep bank, they heard steps in the brush near them.

Had some more of Hooker's gang come down? Maybe they were going to take the bag of stuff and leave the divers without paying them.

Each boy had his own worried thoughts, and they stopped to listen. Again the stealthy steps in the brush. Something was out there, all right. But who was it? Or what?

Hooker yelled, "Hurry up, you creeps! I never saw anybody so slow. Did you find the bag? You'd better!"

"Yes, we found it, but it's heavy," Fins said. "The anchor isn't easy to carry, either."

"How stupid can you be? We don't want the anchor! Just that bag. Cut it loose and come on!"

Fins slashed the anchor rope loose and let it slide back down the bank.

Ahead he could see the shadowy forms of Hooker and Shot Put walking along to meet them; both had a gun hand extended and ready.

Just as Hooker put out his free hand for the bag, a sudden crash came from the brush just back of him.

"Drop those guns! Put up your mitts!" a voice commanded.

Too startled to do anything else, Hooker and Shot Put obeyed. Someone else was in charge now.

Men seemed to pop up from everywhere. The river brush was alive with them! Out of the moving mass of strange faces Fins saw two that meant more to him than any of the others—good old Mel, and Newt Browning. You could count on those guys, both of them!

In a few minutes two officers had Hooker and Shot Put between them in a squad car, while another got the story from Fins and Rich. When that was done, one squad car left. The man who talked to the boys took Rich along with him for more questioning. He had been close to trouble once too often.

Newt brought Fins in his car. Both were worried about Rich and what part he might actually have had in this narcotics ring.

"I think he'll come clean," Fins said. "Rich isn't bad. He just got into some questionable things by accident."

"I understand he's had other such 'accidents,'" Newt answered. "He'd better stop having them or he may someday find himself in just as tight a spot as Hooker and Shot Put. They've taken care of themselves for a long time, but good! Having anything to do with narcotics of any kind is very serious, and it seems they've had plenty to do with it. The papers will probably tell the whole story tomorrow."

Newt was right. The papers had a front-page story on a dope ring broken by the work of a couple of young skin divers and, especially, by the quick thinking of one Fins Harper.

"I'm proud of you, Frank Harper, alias Fins," his mother said. "You'll get along."

16.

UP FOR AIR!

Fins should have been very much excited about
the news stories and the good things people were saying
to and about him. But he wasn't.

Monday night after work, Newt came along and took
him home. Newt left him at his house and drove away.

Fins went in and saw the papers on the table but he
didn't spend much time with them. The front page of the
evening paper carried even more of a story than the morning papers had. All day he'd been hearing about that news
story and his part in breaking the dope ring. He was getting a little tired of it. Anyway, he had things to do now.
Through all this flag-waving he had been doing some solid
thinking.

His mother came in just then.

"Mom," he said, "I'm going back to school. I've already
talked to Mr. Corliss, and he says I can start right away
on trial. I can study at home and take make-up exams, and
by the second semester I'll be up with my class. I called
him from the store today, and we went over everything

I'd have to do. Some of it I won't like, but I think I can take it this time."

"I don't want you to tell me a long story about this, Frank," his mother said, "but what made you change your mind?"

"A lot of things, Mom. I've found out for myself that the diving jobs I want just aren't going to be open to me, even when I'm old enough, unless I learn a lot more about a lot of things. School seems to be the best place to learn those things, even if some of it is pretty stuffy. And I don't want to be hauled in on any more shady diving jobs like these last two. Pay or no pay, I don't want any part of them. So, to keep from being tempted to take that kind, I'd better get ready for the kind I really want. Tomorrow morning I go back to school!"

"What does Mr. Andrews think of this, or have you talked to him yet?" his mother asked.

"He won't care. He's already talked to me a lot about going back to school. A few times I got mad at him for it. He said once I could always work there after school and on Saturdays and vacation times. So that will work out O.K."

Margaret Harper looked at her son with new interest. She couldn't quite remember why she had been so afraid of his skin-diving activities. It seemed silly now.

"Well, Frank," she said, "Fins, I mean, as I said the other night, you'll get along!"

Fins grinned, then turned toward the hall to his room.

"So long, Mom," he said. "I guess I'll go to my room

and dig into that new book on marine science I checked out the other day. It looks pretty good."

Fins went to his room, intending to settle down for a good session with recent books he had checked out on marine science. Idly he turned the pages of one of the latest. It looked good, and he'd get a lot out of it . . . later. But right now there was a restlessness in his blood that good reading wouldn't satisfy.

The late afternoon sun streamed in through the window, made silver flecks on the water of his aquarium. He watched the bright little fish sporting around through the sea grass. Suddenly he knew what he needed! . . . but he had to get a buddy. He started to dial Mel's number, but stopped with the second digit. Mel wouldn't be home. He'd gone to something over at the school.

More than anything else right now, Fins wanted to get to his river. It was a drive more urgent than that of hunger for the good meal he knew his mother was cooking. The pull of the river was a magnet drawing him to it, and against that pull he had little resistance.

But he wouldn't go alone. His suspension from SCUBA had left a lasting impression. Whom could he get to go with him? Newt had classes until nine. That would be too late.

Abruptly another name came to mind. Rich Morton! Maybe he'd go . . . that is, if he was free yet. He dialed Rich's number, and waited.

On the third ring, Rich answered, but not in his usual

half-bragging tone. He was quiet, even subdued. Maybe he needed the river too.

"Hi, Rich! This is Fins. You know . . . that guy . . ."

A sound almost like a gasp at the other end preceded Rich's surprised answer. "I thought you'd be through with me, after what happened the other night."

"Aw, you're not so weird!" Fins replied. "How'd you like to go for a dip in the river?"

"Sure. Lungs?"

"No. Too near suppertime to spend time on a lot of gear. Just the simple stuff. I'll wheel over on my bike."

"Right! Then we'll go in my crate. See you!"

Two receivers clicked, and two boys began gathering snorkel, mask, flippers, and all the rest of it together. If they hurried, they could have nearly an hour's diving before sundown.

Fins checked in at the kitchen.

"I'm going to the river for a few quick dives, Mom. Rich is going with me. O.K.?"

"Sure," she answered. "You can take care of yourself. I'll have dinner ready when you get back."

"O.K. 'Bye, now!"

" 'Bye!"

Fins put his diving things into the bike basket and rolled off toward Rich's home. Rich was waiting, his outfit in the car, and the car running.

The "crate," as Rich called it, was a cheap car of uncertain ancestry, generously decorated with various designs in many wild colors. But Rich prized that car, and it ran, noisily, but with purpose.

"How'd things go for you, Rich?" Fins asked.

Rich needed no fine points brought out. He knew what Fins meant.

"I'm paroled to my parents until the hearing. The officer in charge of the case thinks I'll be on probation for a year. I'm going to night school, too, starting next week."

"What are you doin'? Braggin' or complainin'?" The twinkle in Fins's eyes took the edge off his sharp words.

"Neither. Just telling you. I figure it's a good way to keep from breaking probation. I don't want to go back to high school, though. My class graduated last year."

"What do you want to do . . . for a living, I mean?" Fins asked.

"Auto mechanics. Have my own shop someday, maybe. I'd like to work on crates like this and keep on with diving for fun."

Now they were driving along a stretch of the highway that ran almost along the river bank. The trees grew close and thick, but now and then they caught glimpses of the river.

Rich turned off on the road to the old mine.

"This trip is somewhat different from the one we took last Saturday night," Fins remarked.

"Boy! You said it! I hope I never see those guys again as long as I live!" Rich answered vehemently.

"What I can't understand," Fins remarked, "is how you